NAKED

by
J.T. Pearce.

SILVER MOON BOOKS LTD.
PO Box CR25 Leeds LS7 3TN

Silver Moon Books Inc.
PO Box 1614 New York NY 10156

New Authors Welcome

Printed and bound in Great Britian

Silver Moon Books of Leeds are in no way connected with Silver Moon Books of London

If you like one book you will probably like them all!

A full list of current titles can be found on the back page.

For free 20 page booklet of extracts from previous books (and, if you wish to be on our confidential mailing list, from forthcoming monthly titles as they are published) please write to:-

**Silver Moon Readers Services
PO Box CR 25 LEEDS LS7 3TN
or
PO Box 1614 NEW YORK NY 10156**

NAKED PLUNDER first published in 1997
Copyright Rick Adams
The right of Rick Adams to be identified as author of this book has been asserted in accordance with section 77 and 78 of the Copyrights and Patents Act 1988

NAKED PLUNDER

Rick Adams

BONUS PAGES

Rex Saviour is rewriting and expanding the ever popular but currently out of print
ERICA: PROPERTY OF REX
so as to be enjoyed even by those who have read it before -
and we are serialising it at the end of our next few books
Pages 194-223

This is fiction - in real life, practice safe sex

1

The house Abu took me was at the very edge of the city, past all the poor people's barrios with the bright-eyed nubile women hanging around outside, waiting in the streets for somebody to come and buy their bodies. That's how they made enough money to survive at the edge of Sao Paolo. In the midst of glitter and wealth beyond belief, they sold their flesh, not always necessarily to the highest bidder, for pretty as these girls were, they were also mostly uneducated, and easy to take advantage of in their desperate state.

Abu had dressed me in off-white loose cotton trousers and a loose shirt. He'd insisted I wear a frayed straw hat on my head.

"No good if they see you're rich then master." He winked at me as he said it.

In truth I am no more the master of Abu than I am fabulously wealthy. What I am is a journalist out to do a dirty job and Abu, my childhood friend, was my ticket into the slave trade world I wished to bare to my readers.

"Whatever you see in there," Abu admonished me, "for God's sake say nothing."

Mentally I'd prepared myself for the worst, but nothing could have prepared me for what we encountered when we reached the house.

It was perched high on a hill choked with vegetation, and the outside of it looked flimsy enough. It gave the appearance of having been constructed of dark wood and cheap brick. The truth however became more apparent the closer we approached.

"Good evening master Sahim," Abu yelled into the shadows by the gate.

A fierce looking black man emerged. A large machine gun hung from his shoulder. "Who's that with you Abu?" he asked eyeing me with great suspicion.

"Ask no impertinent questions and you shall receive no falsehood," Abu said cheerfully. "The master with me is not for naming. Has the show began inside?"

The guard hesitated for a moment, obviously weighing the options available to him, then he consulted his watch. "You're right on time, it's starting any minute now."

"Be on your guard then master Sahim." Abu waved a benevolent hand towards the brute. "There's no telling what unwanted elements may wish to grace us inside if you let them." And with that we slipped past the big metal gates and found ourselves on the grounds of a big villa.

I could now see that the impression of a little house upon a hill was a cleverly constructed fake, much like a purpose-built movie set, and could admire the ingenuity of the builder.

"Not a word now, mind you. Or both our lives will hang on a thread," Abu hissed, and taking me firmly by the elbow he led me inside.

I followed Abu to a huge semi-darkened room. The windows were shut, the blinds drawn to keep out prying eyes, and a quiet air-conditioner piped out the Brazilian heat.

When my eyes became accustomed to the gloom I noticed that the edges of the room were strewn with chairs. Men dressed much as myself occupied these chairs, and scantily clad mulatto girls circulated freely between them, passing the men drinks and thick cigars in the manner of usherettes.

One of these girls passed right in front of me, her short tunic bobbing merrily at the front, evidence, if I needed any, to the fact that her nubile breasts rode unfettered.

I smelt her scent, a mixture of juniper and jasmine, and then she was past, her round dark eyes downcast, her long black hair drawn back to show off her slender neck and fine chocolate coloured features.

The sleeveless tunics these girls wore were short. Barely preserving their modesty. As I followed the girl with my eyes I saw her stop and curtsy quickly before a bald corpulent looking man and offer him a thick cigar from the tray she held in her hands.

The man nodded imperceptibly and as the girl bent to light the cigar for him his thick-fingered white hands crawled up the backs of the girl's shapely thighs and hefted a plump round buttock.

The girl's short tunic had ridden high enough as she bent forward to reveal her complete lack of underwear.

I watched fascinated as the fat man's roving hand squeezed and kneaded the girl's pliant buttocks and then, before my very eyes, moved to the tender lips of her open sex, and inserted a thick index finger inside her vulva.

In all this time the girl did not so much as flinch. She finished lighting the fat man's cigar, waited patiently for him to extract his finger from her, and the minute this was done, with a suggestive swing of her hips, eyes still downcast, she went on her way, to ask the next man if he would like a cigar.

I counted eight of these girls making the rounds, willowy exotic usherettes offering both cigars and drink.

"Drink nothing from here," Abu hissed by my side. "Half the time the drinks are drugged, and the cigars are so strong they'll make you sick."

A young girl stopped before us. She too wore a short tunic and judging by the fine lithe lines of her young figure, I judged she couldn't have been more than nineteen.

"Cigar young masters?" she asked, and I could see she meant it. The language of masters and slaves, which Abu sometimes playfully employed, was here spoken for real.

"Not for us." Abu waved her away, but before she could

depart, a devil possessed me. It was not often I was given the chance to see close up such fine girls being so easily available. Mesmerised with temptation, I reached out and put my hand on her left knee. Instantly the girl froze.

Intrigued how far I could push it, unable to believe that I could have such power to make a girl stop and submit just by a simple touch, I let my hand travel up her left thigh. I caressed the smooth silk of her inner thigh, going up, under her tunic to the junction between her legs.

Her sex, I felt, was depilated, its smooth round lips slightly raised. Entranced by the girl's young beauty, her inability to raise her eyes, I stroked her between her legs, gently pushed open her nether lips, parted them with my fingers. My crotch in response was tight with arousal. The front of the loose white trousers I wore ballooned in a way that was impossible to hide.

The girl bit her bottom lip. Small white even teeth left tiny indentations in the dark cherry coloured flesh and it is only then that I noticed that Abu, even as I invaded with a finger the moist coral depths of the girl's sex, had parted the tight round cheeks of her ass and had inserted his own calloused digit into the tight bud of her anus.

"Let her be," he said with a wicked glint in his eye when he noticed I'd discovered him. "There'll be better sport to be had later if you have a mind to, and besides the show's about to begin."

Indeed, even as he spoke a gong sounded from the depths of the house somewhere. Instantly an air of transformation came over all the men seated in the room. On cue, the young girls withdrew to their assigned positions by the walls and a spotlight lit the centre of that cavernous hall.

From a doorway I had not noticed, a dark haired man, about my age, impeccably dressed and carrying a wireless microphone, took centre stage.

"Gentlemen!" He addressed the gathering with a fine flourish.

"That's Mr Soames," Abu whispered urgently by my side.

I straightened up immediately. So this was the legendary Edward Soames, a native of England reputed to be on the run for some heinous crime no one had discovered. I watched him turn to take in the men, his eyes quickly surveying the positions the girls had taken up. I noticed then more figures, strategically placed in the shadows. Figures more reminiscent of the Neanderthal guarding the gate downstairs than of the willowy girls who served cigars and alcohol.

"Good to see so many of you tonight," Soames continued. "It is good to take such active interest in the welfare of our less fortunate citizens. Rescuing them from poverty and starvation. Offering them the chance to enjoy a different life. A more gracious one, perhaps." He stopped here and surveyed us all, read the fever pitch of excitement in our eyes, and must have smelled the animal smell of our primitive lust.

I was not fooled by his words, aroused though I was. I knew them for the justification these wealthy magnates used for the depravities they practised upon the nubile flesh of the unwilling barrio girls they so illegally bought here.

"There are some of you here tonight I have never seen before. Perhaps afterwards, if you could be so kind as to indulge me I would like a very brief word." His eyes were directed at me when he spoke, and I suddenly felt chills run down my spine.

Although officially nothing had ever been found against Soames, he had a reputation for being ruthless, and I already knew of one case of a journalist who had been inconsiderate enough to pry too deeply into this man's affairs.

"And now, let tonight's show begin!" and with that he clapped his hands.

Immediately the lights fell even lower. Artificial smoke

was piped in from somewhere and as if by magic a beautiful cluster of young girls appeared in the very middle of the room.

They were all of mixed blood, their fine features and smooth limbs the colour of burnished sandalwood, tinged with the barest hint of chocolate.

Ethereal music piped in from somewhere and the girls started slowly to undulate their bodies to its oriental rhythms.

Whereas the usherettes had been dressed in short sleeveless tunics, each with a different motif adorned on it, the girls I saw now were dressed in scraps of clothing, like they'd just been picked up from the street.

The glowing sheen of their finely washed long hair, the healthy appearance of their long limbs, lent as much a lie to this fact as the strategically placed rips in their clothing.

They were all barefoot and dressed in full ankle length skirts and a cropped top that left their midriff bare.

Rips and tears in their skirts and tops gave tantalising glimpses of their bodies as they danced. There would be the flare of a young thigh glimpsed through a long rent in a wide peasant skirt, the suggestive curve of tight young buttocks, the darkened thrust of a nippled mound of flesh.

In the midst of them all a bull-headed man moved like a primitive animal. His body was square and squat, his head shaved completely. In one hand he carried a riding crop, and as the girls danced and swirled about him, he would use it to flick a long skirt up, revealing a slim leg to the very top of its thigh. Or he would take hold of a girl, her willowy body looking suddenly very fragile in his meaty grip, and to the onlooker's expressed delight he would slip a rough hand under her top, begin to heft and squeeze her firm breasts.

The girl would stoically bear this, unresisting, though an expression of terror and distaste would creep into her face, and this would drive the white-clad gentlemen wild.

I noticed then the subtle hand-signals. The slight nods.

And saw how clear across the room stood Soames, by a gigantic black board, chalk in hand, and as the nods and hand-signals came in, a young assistant would whisper them to him, and up would go some numbers. Numerical values assigned beside each name. The names being those of the dancing girls. The numbers being the prices different masters were thus bidding for them.

I kept my hands on my lap, unwilling to participate in this debasement of young girls, even to maintain my cover. My eyes were firmly riveted on the brute amidst the dancing girls, and I saw now how artful was his act, for as the prices mounted, the bidding frenzy took hold, so was he emboldened and by design descended into new levels of lewdness.

His riding crop cut the air, the girls around him, quickened their step in response, cavorted and gyrated more frantically, but this was all part of the design. Their increased alacrity would not save them.

With a cobra-like motion the brute grabbed a girl. She was an exceptional beauty. The exertion of the dance had made her cheeks flash and had brought the sheen of vitality to her young face, and as the brute caught her the erotic effect was accentuated by the undisguised terror in her eyes.

The rest of the girls kept on twisting, throwing their skirts up as they span, showing everybody the long, sexy lines of their legs, throwing their hair forward and then flicking it back, making their breasts jiggle beneath their cropped tops. But it was to the caught girl that every man's eyes in that room now centred.

The brute sensed this and judged his moment finely, waiting for the oriental tune and the girls' dance to reach a crescendo, and as this happened he turned the girl, a firm hand round her slim waist, to face the circle of onlookers.

"Please," the girl's lips silently whispered, but the brute was inured to such pleadings.

With his free hand he raked her skirt up, bunched it around her slender waist, and forced her to kneel on hands and knees, facing away from him.

The round cheeks of the girl's full backside were revealed to us all.

"Watch this," Abu said to me from my side. The excitement evident on his face made me think that he'd seen what was to come before, and more, he even approved of it.

With her backside exposed, her sex vulnerably open, the girl tried to take sudden flight, to crawl away from the man who held her. But the brute had expected this. With one firm hand he grabbed her hair. Pulled her head back. Displayed to us all her fine, young features. The full lips, the languid, liquid eyes, now so full of terror. With his other he tore at her flimsy dress ripped the skirt off her body, pulled at the cropped top she had on her back.

The girl's naked body was now displayed in all its glorious beauty. Already I could see Soames, in the background, scribbling furiously against a name, MELLISA, and almost astronomical numbers being written next to it.

Melissa, if that was her real name, tried vainly to hide the fulsome bounty of her exposed breasts with one hand across her chest. In vain. The instant she did that, the brute behind her whipped her across the full round buttocks with his riding crop. The impact was audible even above the tunes of the oriental music and the effect was obvious.

The cheeks of Melissa's buttocks shook. Her head shot back, eyes now awash in pain as well as terror. The hand she held across her chest fell away and her round full breasts fell free, their dark nippled tips, engorged with pain, stood out tightly against the burnished background of her flesh.

The display made those around me go wild. They half rose out of their seats, ignoring the rest of the dancing girls, their voices hoarse with excitement.

"Again, again, hit her again."

"Plough those sweet rear mounds for us."

"Give it to her."

And the brute complied. He raised his hand to full swing, the riding crop held high, and then brought it swinging down, raising a red welt across the girl's full buttocks, less than an inch above the one his previous stroke had marked.

He could have gone like that for some time, for he obviously enjoyed this part of his work, but a quick glance at his master was enough to let the brute know that the girl was fast approaching the maximum of her potential value.

Something extra was required to raise the bidding the final distance.

Grabbing the girl by the back of the head, the brute pushed her face down towards the plush carpet. Grateful not to be hit again, she lay with her head held low, cradled in her arms, the round cheeks of her ass on show, the tight bud of her anus and the open depilated lips of her cunt clearly visible to the onlookers.

With a quick chopping motion of his left hand the brute made the dancing girls stop. At his bidding they each sat on the floor, forming a rough circle around the naked Melissa, prostate now on the floor, her ass raised vulnerably to the brute standing behind her.

The music stopped.

We all watched with bated breath as the brute changed his grip upon the riding crop, not one of us not secretly wishing to change places with him. He held the riding crop now so that the long slender handle of it pointed threateningly towards the vulnerable orifices the girl's posture so openly displayed.

"Gentlemen, what am I bid for her?" Soames called out from the far end of the room. "Place your final bids now!" And at a nod from him, the brute behind Melissa pushed the handle of the riding crop between her legs, smoothly parted the raised lips of her sex and gave us all a brief glimpse of succulent pink folds before the handle of the riding crop was engulfed within them.

Melissa, head down, let out a moan, and her hips rolled a little. Apart from that she made no other reaction.

"A magnificent animal, gentlemen, an asset to any man's life," Soames said as the bidders went frantic.

The brute left the riding crop where it was, but, of his own accord now, slid his hands over the smooth round globes of the girl's ass. He caressed them with unexpected gentleness, then suddenly slapped her, first with one hand, then with the other, making her cheeks tremble, the reddening imprint of his thick hand visible to most buyers.

Melissa cried out in response, a muffled cry at this new assault, and to my shame I found myself aroused by this display. Her beautiful ripe body, submissive, available to any use a man could dream to put it to.

The punters beside me and all around went near hysterical. They rose out of their chairs, waved straw hats at Soames, handkerchiefs, even shoes.

Sensing the success of his actions, the brute now withdrew the riding crop, making Melissa's hips roll again. Its end, as it came out her body, was glistening with her fluids, and I can swear that every man in that room was imagining what it would be like to stick their cocks inside her and make her cry out with passion.

The brute wasn't yet finished. He played the glistening end of the riding crop upon the girl's flesh, first moving it down the length of one inside thigh, almost to the floor, then sliding it up the other, and then suddenly as he slid it past her open sex, he stopped, arrested its movement.

Poised above her bottom.

There was instant silence. We could all read his intent

and waited. The brute looked around teasingly, and then with a grin that bared all his teeth he drove the poised end of the riding crop against the tightly closed button of the girl's anus.

Melissa's head flew up, her mouth opened to cry out in direct response to the pain that was being inflicted upon her flesh, but at the last possible moment, Soames cried: "Enough! We have a buyer."

The brute stopped, disappointment at not having been able to ram his riding crop deep enough up Melissa's ass evident on his blunt face.

A couple of effeminate looking men, dressed in orange, suddenly appeared and, wrapping a red robe around Melissa's body, helped lift her to her feet and quickly whisked her away.

The rest of the girls followed the two men, heads down, shuffling their feet, ashamed at having failed to arouse enough interest in their prospective masters.

The usherettes once more started circulating amongst us. Their charms, however, now looked very tame compared to what we had just witnessed, and not many men seemed interested.

"Time to go?" Abu asked. I detected a note of anxiety in his voice. "It would not do to overstay. Soames can be a nasty bastard if he suspects he's being set up and -"

At that exact minute a door opened just behind us. Soames stood momentarily silhouetted in its frame, the massive bulk of the brute who'd just used Melissa, stood just behind him.

"Mr Sinhail!" He addressed Abu first. "Mr Lewis!" He called me by my real name. "Feel yourselves my guests. Malakai here will show you your quarters."

The brute stepped forward.

Abu and I exchanged a quick look of apprehension.

Then, thinking that things might not be as unsalvageable as they seemed, I stood up slowly and replied: "Thank you, Mr Soames."

But the door behind us had shut as quickly and quietly as it had opened, and Malakai stood there, arms folded, looking like a man who would derive just as much pleasure out of killing us as he had out of his use of Melissa.

We followed him to a big room. One with sturdy bars at the windows, with a view to a carefully cultivated garden, patrolled by big men with guns and dogs. And hardened though I was to danger, I admit that at that moment even I had doubts as to whether we would come out of this little caper with our lives.

"He must have known about you," Abu whispered the minute Malakai left us alone. "But at least we won't starve." He pointed to a table heavily laden with fruit and crystal decanters full of whisky.

"What if it's drugged?" I asked, mindful still of his admonition earlier that evening.

Abu looked at me and he shrugged. "It hardly matters now. If they mean us harm there's little we can do to prevent it. You saw how many of them there are, and they're all armed."

He was right of course. We made ourselves comfortable. The exotic fruits were ripe and the whisky of exceptional quality.

"Perhaps they'd let us have one last fling, before they do away with us," Abu said, refilling his glass and mine. "Those girls, my God they were beautiful! What wouldn't I give to plough my seed into their sweet fields."

His words made me think again of Melissa. The haunting quality of her beauty, the exquisite body, the other-worldly charms. The whisky made me feel more relaxed, a lot less inhibited than I would normally be and I am sure Abu felt its effects in exactly the same manner, for I asked him there and then if he had ever traded in human flesh.

He paused for a moment and looked at me. "We've been

friends a long ti...
haven't got many secre...
could you resist?"

I should perhaps have been shock...
hood friend admitting to being an occasion...
One of those who took advantage of the poor and le...
nate in our society. But I was also intrigued.

"What are they like?"

Abu looked wistfully at the ceiling. "Best fuck a man can have. Submissive. Willing to please in any way." He caught my eye then and gave me one of his rare smiles. "I didn't keep them long of course. You'll find once you've tasted honey from the honeypot you just want to come back for more. Variety indeed is the spice of life, my friend."

"What did you do with them?" I asked, almost too horrified to hear the answer.

"Nothing of what you might expect," he said. "I gave them each $5,000, found them a suitable match, or, if that's what they wished, I saw them safely to their village."

I felt relieved. Whatever vileness was being perpetrated on these unfortunate young souls, Abu had little enough part to play in it, and as for his weakness who was I to judge? Less than an hour earlier I had felt the sweet cunt of a young usherette, entranced by her submissive beauty, and had we been alone I was sure that I would have been persuaded by my desire to go further.

Just then the door opened and Malakai walked in.

We would have stood up, normally, but the drink and fruit and candid talk had worked their magic and Abu and I were determined that whatever our end would be we would face it together, like true gentlemen, without loss of dignity.

Malakai came to a stop directly in front of us. He put massive hands on his belt and asked "Enjoyin' de whisky?"

"It is not as bad as some, though Highlands single-malt it

...... from his reclined position.

... words had little effect on the brute, who continued to stare at us impassively. "Get up," he said to Abu, "Mr Soames wants to speak to you."

"You'd better go," I said as he hesitated, and watched him stand up, a little unsteady on his feet.

"Divide and rule," Abu whispered as he went by me. It occurred to me then that the two of us could have a go at overpowering Malakai, making a break for it, but drunk as we were, it was possible the brute would be a match for us, and there was no guarantee he didn't have other henchmen standing as back up just outside the heavy wooden door.

So I let him pass by my feet, leading Abu by an elbow and heard the door close behind them.

I felt guilty, responsible for whatever harm might befall my friend. And to ease my inner suffering I emptied the last of the crystal decanter in my glass and with a quick jerk of the head poured it down my throat.

I closed my eyes and felt the burning passage of the fiery liquid calm my nerves. Abu was a grown man, I reasoned. I hadn't forced him to take me along, he'd done it as a favour.

When the sting of the drink had faded and I opened my eyes I saw Melissa standing in front of me.

I stared uncomprehendingly. It was a Melissa transformed. Her long black hair had been piled on top of her head in an elaborate knot. Her eyes and lips were expertly made up and she wore a simple white dress that left the enticing swell of the tops of her breasts uncovered. Through the thin fabric I could see the round dark circles of her proud nipples, the firm swell of her breasts. The simple dress fell to her waist where it was held by a wide belt of tanned leather, and ended just above her knees.

Her feet were encased in leather sandals, the sort that laced up halfway up the calf. Irresistibly my eyes were drawn to the long slits of her dress on either side. They went up her legs, exposing the fullness of each thigh and stopped at the hip.

Even in my alcohol befogged state I could see she had no underwear. A brief image of her naked body flashed in my mind and made my pulse speed up.

"I must be dreaming," I mumbled, and made to get off my recliner.

"It's no dream Mr Lewis," she said. Her English was flawless. Her voice was soft, throaty, with hints of suppressed passion in its every note.

"I didn't hear the door."

"There are more doors in this place than walls," she said, then falling to her knees in front of me she took my hand, "are you sober enough to understand?"

"You were sold," I mumbled. "I saw you being sold."

"I am no more for sale than you are Mr Lewis," she said. "I am Edward's private chattel. For his exclusive use alone."

She said this quickly. Her impassioned eyes briefly met mine. Fell away again.

I felt the blanket of drunkenness recede from my mind and instantly took in the import of this confession. I shut up, cupped her beautifully shaped chin in one hand and tilted her head until her eyes once again were on mine.

"You mean tonight's show -"

"Oh that was real enough," she interrupted. "Edward loves seeing Malakai abuse me in public. But you must have noticed the large sums paid for me. The way the bidding kept on going higher and higher until it went too high for most of them to afford me."

I nodded that I had.

"That's Edward's doing. The man bidding for me is his own. There was not a single man there who could have outbidden him."

"But no other girl was sold!"

"Not then, no. Who would want to admit that having failed to obtain the best girl they'd go for a second-best one? But afterwards it got them thinking. Until the moment Malakai tore my clothes off, I had been just one more girl in the troupe. Believe me Mr Lewis there's not a single girl in that troupe who is not with a buyer tonight."

I believed her. Her tone was sincere. And the information she had just given me added a new twist to Soames' game, though what I would do with it, given my current predicament, was hard to say.

"Why are you telling me all this?"

"Mr Lewis, you are a journalist, Mr Soames fears your power. If anyone could help me break free of this man's bonds, it has to be you."

She delivered this with a conviction of voice that instantly put me on guard. It was evident to me that I was in no position to help anybody right now and as for Soames fearing me, that was surely a jest. Soames feared no man. But it could be he wanted to enjoy some sport with me and this girl here was sent to entrap me in some elaborate trap.

"How do I know I can trust you?" I asked rising from my recliner. I noticed that she had remained on her knees still, and was now kneeling in front of me, her beautiful face looking up at me.

Without taking her liquid dark eyes off mine her hands dropped to her slender waist and she quickly undid the thick leather belt she wore there.

Before I could stop her, she'd slipped the thin straps of her dress from her shoulders with one languid motion and slid it down around her knees.

She was totally naked.

Her eyes implored mine. "Soames' use of me is not only sexual," she said in that soft, purry voice of hers. She raised her hands to her flat abdomen where etched on the magnificent skin were raw thick welts the width of the belt she wore. "I really cannot take it any more Mr Lewis. You are my last hope. I will do anything, anything to get away from him and this place."

She dropped her eyes as she said this and made no attempt to hide her nudity.

The invitation was obvious in her posture and voice. I stood there undecided, the alcohol I had consumed now making it hard to think. Undoubtedly she was a magnificent animal. Seeing her so submissive and vulnerable, on her knees in front of me, stirred passions in my breast that I would normally fight hard rather than admit to.

But my current state of mind, the strange things I had just heard, the drink I'd consumed and the talk I had had with Abu, about having a girl before we died. In fact, the very imminent possibility, that indeed my fate was sealed. It all conspired to rob me of my normal sensibilities and with a violent grasp I took hold of her sleek, dark hair and forced her head back.

So forced was she to violent behaviour that my act seemed more a caress to her and she let out a small sigh.

Holding her thus, with my free hand I pulled open the front of my trousers and extracted my erect cock, the head swollen and almost purple with lust.

I wanted to have all of this girl now. I longed to fling myself on top of her and taste the fruits of her beautiful breasts. I wanted to feel the soft belly beneath me, the tender thighs open, yielding to my demands. I ached to grasp the twin moons of her buttocks and crash them in my hands just like Malakai had earlier, and so publicly done. But at the back of my mind was the very real possibility that all of this was just a trap. That time was shortening even as I stood there and I had to avail myself of her as fast as I could.

So instead, I stepped forward and pulling her face towards my waist thrust my cock into her mouth.

With a barely audible moan, Melissa took it all in. I thrust my hips forward and felt it go deeper, tickle the very back of her throat and she almost gagged.

"Suck it bitch! Suck it deeper!" I whispered with urgency pulling her face towards me, so that her chin was scrunched against the wiry locks at the base of my manhood.

I was beyond myself with lust. There was something about the place, the girl, that made me forget all of who I was and what I had gone there to do, and all I wanted now was to have her suck me as hard and as deep as was possible.

It is indicative of the level of abuse this beautiful creature was used to that she found my deplorably ungentlemanly behaviour, my barely suppressed level of violence, an almost tender act.

She opened her mouth wide to swallow me. Her tongue circled round the head of my glans and then she pulled back until I almost popped out of her soft mouth, her lips tightened their hold around me and with the tip of her tongue I felt her explore the opening of my pisshole.

With her left hand she cupped my scrotum and she began gently to squeeze in a rhythmic, soft motion. It was more than I could take.

With a gasp I stiffened. My hips drove forward, spasming involuntarily and I shot my seed, felt it splash into her willing mouth.

Her eyes on me, Melissa, drunk every spurt. She worked her mouth and lips, taking it all in. Swallowing it, sucking it in, just like I had told her to.

Presently I finished and withdrew from her mouth with disgust at myself and my behaviour.

"Will you take me with you?" she implored.

My eyes roamed over her full breasts. I realised then that

I had not yet had my fill of her beauty and grasping her hair again, I pulled her roughly to her feet, wrapped my arms round her willowy waist and buried my face between her breasts.

I drunk in the sweet scent of them. I browsed upon the firmness of her pliant orbs. I suckled on the tightening nipples and my hands explored her body. Marched up and down the lithe smoothness of her back. Hefted and squeezed her plump round buttocks.

I would have done more. A lot more. But just then we both heard the unmistakeable tread of a man's step at the door.

"I must go!" Melissa pushed me gently away. Quickly she bent down to pick up her dress and leather belt from the floor as I fumbled to fix the front of my trousers.

There was the sound of a turning key at the door. This was it, the trap was being sprang at last.

Out of the corner of one eye I saw Melissa dart towards the far wall. And then the door opened and Edward Soames, dressed in casual grey slacks, white loafers and a navy blue jacket, came in.

"Are you bored, Mr Lewis?" he asked.

"Er, no," I mumbled. I half turned around but of Melissa there was no sign. I thought I noticed a drapery at the far wall sway ever so slightly, but I couldn't be sure.

"You must forgive me this little charade with Malakai," he said, "but Mr Sinhail was with you. Mr Sinhail is a good customer of mine and his opinion counts and I wouldn't want to disillusion him as to the effectiveness of my security measures."

"What have you done with Abu?" I asked. The thought of Abu brought my courage back. If this monster had hurt him, I swore, I would revenge his death even if it killed me.

"Mr Sinhail has gone home, though not without some

protestation from him and quite a lot of assurances from me regarding your safety."

"You let him go?" I could hardly believe my ears.

"Oh, come now, Mr Lewis," Soames chuckled, "We're civilised people here. There is no need for violence as long as we understand where each of us stands."

"Meaning?"

He met my eye. "Meaning that I assured Mr Sinhail of your safety, but I also told him that for a few days at least you would be my guest here."

"You'd make a prisoner of me?"

"Oh, nothing so dramatic. You'll have the free run of the place and - its services. But you'll be forbidden any contact with the outside world for three days. After the three days are over you'll be free to go wherever you like, meet whomever you please and write whatever you like."

"Why three days?"

He smiled. "If I can't convince you in that time that what goes on here is less vile than you think, and a sight better than the alternatives some of our girls face on the outside, the chances are I never will."

"Is this a game?" I asked.

"Consider it a challenge. Forget about sensationalist coverage and newspaper circulation figures for an instant. Forget about inflated libertarian ideals which have more root in a utopian dreamworld than in the present. This is the 20th century. Think up an argument that would convince me that what I do for these girls is wrong."

"Selling them?"

"Facilitating their passage into a better life. A life infinitely superior to what they have enjoyed until now."

"Very well then, it's a deal," I said.

"Excellent, excellent, I knew you wouldn't be able to resist the challenge. One does get so bored this far from England you know Mr Lewis. I'm so glad you did come," and with that Edward Soames stepped forward and shook my hand, clinching our strange agreement.

"Malakai." He clicked his fingers at the door behind him. "Get Mr Lewis some clothes."

I watched Malakai's bulk hurry off to carry out his master's orders and thought how strange. How strange that I should strike a deal with the very man I had come to expose. But the memory of hot soft lips sucking my cock still remained. And in truth, I now looked forward to renewing my acquaintance with the exquisite Melissa.

2

It was a strange situation to find oneself in, I admit. An exotic environment full of fresh girls who could be had for one's own use, at short notice.

I thought of Soames' strange proposition, the strange deal we'd struck, and wondered even at my own sense of sanity.

The sheer speed at which everything had happened, the maddening lust that seemed to grip hold of me every time my thoughts returned to Melissa - her perfect body, her willing mouth - it all proved too much even for me to take in my stride.

Looking back I see now that the entire tableau had been carefully orchestrated by the Englishman from the very beginning. It was to serve as a means to intoxicate me and unbalance my good judgement more than his whisky had ever done. And in that respect, I must say, it succeeded admirably.

It was my intention from the very first moment, of course, to ensure the right thing was done. To make certain the odious character of Soames received the justice he deserved and the poor unfortunates who found themselves sold into sexual servitude were released from their unlawful bonds and freed from his grasp.

That things did not go exactly as I planned them is testimony perhaps to the nature of the fact. The adage I now know as true: the road to hell, indeed, is paved with good intentions. But I digress, for at that moment, poor though my situation seemed to be, I felt that at least my plan was beginning to work.

I really felt that I would easily escape the evil Englishman's clutches and with the help of my boyhood friend, Abu, who I was certain would not abandon me, I would find a way to expose his evil ways.

My thoughts were interrupted again by heavy footsteps. True to his master's orders the hulking Malakai, his sullen visage not least softened by my apparent rise in his master's favours, had fetched me some decent clothes. Black cotton trousers, crisply ironed. A white shirt, open at the throat, and a white linen jacket.

He laid these out on the table in front of me and stood back, thick, powerful arms crossed across his forbidding chest.

To lay appear naked before a stranger would normally give me feelings of vulnerability. But I was caught at the time in the spirit of the game Soames had so cleverly instigated and was determined to prove that I was, at least, his equal.

If he thought to intimidate me through his brutish servant's presence I would prove him wrong. So I stripped and stood there in my white skin and naked body unflinching. I turned my back to the brute, ignoring him as if he wasn't there, and picked up the clothes he'd brought.

I felt, as I put them on, like a man reborn. Shedding my old skin. Putting on a new identity. An identity I did not completely yet control and of which even now I am as yet unsure of. Malakai watched me impassively as I dressed, his face completely inscrutable.

Be damned to him! Whatever the nature of my deal with Soames I decided I would best him, at his own game.

And publish my story exposing him.

I was determined.

"Where do I sleep? Or is that not allowed here?" I asked the silent brute, but before he could answer his master's voice spoke up.

"Sleep will come later. I want to show you something first."

I turned round to see Soames standing by the shadows behind us. I hadn't seen him enter. Distracted as I was by my sudden change of fortune and my own thoughts, his sudden appearance rattled me.

He gave me a devilish smile and without bothering to explain his sudden appearance bade for me to follow him.

As we went past Malakai I caught a dark look this vicious brute cast our way, and so venomous was its aspect that I momentarily felt all new-found bravado flee my body and my heart fluttered with terror at the prospect of what might lie ahead for me.

"There are not many people like you who come to my house Frank. I may call you Frank?"

I nodded my ascent. I followed Soames silently listening to his professed loneliness, so far from Europe, and I wondered afresh on the nature of his crimes that he was thus sentenced to such self-imposed exile. His voice was smooth and cultured as he took me past more doors than I thought his villa could possibly have.

"We have had to be ingenious here, of course," he said. "We've tunnelled far back into the hillside behind us, we've expanded unseen and without having to pay the graft that would have surely been demanded of us. What I have built here is a pleasure dome. Like the one mentioned in Xanadu, the famous Coleridge poem. A man may come here to experience his most forbidden dreams. His most secret desires."

As he spoke, he lowered the tone of his voice to just above a whisper and indicated that I should likewise do the same, if I needed to talk at all.

He then reached out, touched an ornate lamp situated in the corridor, about shoulder height, and stepped back.

An entire section of the wall slid back on silent hinges to reveal a long dark passage.

"Come. Say nothing. I have not yet had the time to soundproof all the mirrors and sound carries well down here."

Mystified, I followed him silently, blinking to help my eyes adjust. We were in a narrow corridor that must pass behind the rooms, the closed doors of which we'd just gone past.

Each room had a two way mirror installed, and was is through these that we were now afforded the most explicit view of what was going on within. It was like standing in front of secret windows and looking into the deepest and most forbidden desires of those on the other side.

Soames stopped and peered through the first mirror. His features were barely visible in the feeble light that seeped in from the room beyond, but even in that poor light I could see an unhealthy, scheming fascination creep into his eyes as he watched what was going on within.

Standing beside him, in the dark, I was beginning to feel a tinge of curiosity myself. The journalist within me was getting impatient with Soames' antics, but as it turned out I didn't have to wait in that manner for long, for moments later the Englishman motioned for me to follow his example and peer through the mirror at the world beyond.

I had to struggle hard to refrain from uttering a gasp of indignation. I had expected the worst. Soames, once again, had not disappointed me.

There, on the other side of the mirror was the mayor of the city, a corpulent man I had seen in public on more than one occasion, but never like this.

The man was naked to the waist, the front of his trousers bulging with the thickness of his aroused erection. In his right hand he held a braided whip. The length of it was polished to a shiny blackness, its stock thick, the tip tapering to a wicked thinness that spoke of frequent use.

He flexed the whip in both hands, this way and that, warming up the length of it, sliding his hands up and down it in a slow caress that became all the more indecent to me the moment I spied the object of his attention.

Directly in front of the Mayor was a low table, fashioned of rough-hewn wood and approximately square in shape. The table itself was bare of adornment of any description, which was strange because the room itself, what little I could see of it from where I stood, was expensively done, in thick velvets and furs.

But what most caught my attention was the tied-up figure that lay on the table.

She was a willowy brown girl, in a thin white, cotton dress the hem of which reached all the way down to her ankles. She had been bent over so that her face lay flat on the tabletop and her arms had been stretched to either side of her and tied with silk to the legs of the table in a parody of the crucifixion.

She had very long black hair that fell in tight ringlets about her shoulders and face. It hid her features from me and created a pleasing contrast against the brilliant white of her simple dress.

Tied, as she was, like that, I noticed that she was barefoot. Her body was pulled forward too far, rendering her helpless, so that she had to stand on tip-toe to relieve the pressure from her arms.

Through the thin white cotton of her simple dress, I could see the faintest outline of her body. And as she breathed in and out the suggestive outline of her hips rose and fell in an indecently inviting manner.

The mayor had finished warming the polished whip now. and I saw him approach the girl. When he stood but two feet from her, he viciously cut the air above her body with the whip, making the very tip of it produce a thunderous crack. In instant response the prostate girl's body wriggled helplessly against her bonds.

She rose and fell on the tips of her toes, tried to move her head but failed. As she moved her body in that fashion I could have sworn that beneath that thin white dress, the clean, outline of her body spoke of the fact that the girl was naked. That indeed all the mayor would have to do was flip the hem of her cotton dress up and expose the twin cheeks of her round ass beautifully framing the sensitive centre of her, there for him to use as he saw fit.

He cracked the whip again, and again the girl wriggled.

Her wriggling made the dress bunch up a little beneath her, so that the hem rode up the backs of her legs exposing the firm line of her calves and the backs of her knees. Pulled up like that, the dress moulded itself against the arousing width of her hips, stretching the material across her buttocks and drawing attention to the dark outline of the deep cleavage between the cheeks of her ass.

Despite her provocative helplessness and all her wriggling, not once had the girl cried out, which meant that she was familiar with what was expected of her, and had, possibly, even been especially prepared.

In my sojourns as a journalist through the illicit houses where my informers were expected to be frequently found, I had heard enough of tales of girls being gang-raped to better prepare them for just this sort of use.

The shock of such treatment, as had been explained to me, helped numb the girl's fear of pain and made her even more responsive to sensations she may have otherwise found unwelcome.

The truth or falsehood of such claims was not for me to judge, but as I watched fascinated the young unfortunate lying on the other side of the mirror I had to admit to myself that her ripe young flesh, straining against its bonds they way she was, was crying out to be used.

It was obvious that the Mayor had done this kind of thing before. He had a practised ease with which he used the whip, careful, at this stage, not to mark the girl. And he revelled in the obvious power he exercised over her.

Having finished playing with the whip, the mayor now came up close behind the girl. He stood so until the tip of his bulging penis almost brushed against the thinly clothed curve of her vulnerable buttocks.

The instant the girl felt his presence so close to her, her whole body stretched out. She pulled hard against her bonds, so that the clean thin lines of her arms and back were obvious through her thin dress, and her haunches seductively curved and vulnerably presented, arched and raised themselves against the table, further adding to the allure of her form.

Mesmerised, I watched as the Mayor dropped a hand to the hem of the girl's thin dress and slowly pulled it upwards, revealing, inch by painful inch, the smooth line of her thighs and then the tightly clenched clefts of her bare buttocks.

Involuntarily, the girl cried out at this, and wriggled once more, and although I could not see her face, the sound of her voice and the clean freshness of her skin confirmed for me that my original guess had been right and she could be no more than nineteen or so.

The mayor finished pulling the girl's dress up. He bunched

it up around her hips and stepped back to admire the view her exposed rear presented him with.

Unsure as yet of what form of assault this man planned to perpetrate upon her, the girl pulled her knees close together. She wriggled her ass and tried to protect the vulnerable opening of her as much as possible.

Her wriggling had exactly the opposite effect. As she pulled her knees together, so that they almost touched, her tight haunches arched even higher off the table top. The tight button of her anus winked at me and the vertical line of her sex opened to show me the tender pink folds within. I fancied I spied the barest glint of a trace of a pearl-shaped droplet of moisture within those folds and involuntarily, in the dark, I wet my lips in anticipation.

I was quite aware of the fact that despite my inner sense of outrage at the fate this unfortunate was about to suffer, such was the beauty of her that I had become secretly aroused. The throb of my penis made itself felt against the tightness of the trousers I wore, and for once I felt grateful for the darkness which now cloaked us.

Satisfied with what he was seeing, the mayor now stepped back. He raised his arm, the whip held ready. Then, with a sweeping, arcing motion, he brought its thin length down. The whip's end wrapped itself round the bound girl's exposed buttocks, momentarily clinging to them like a black, coiled snake.

The girl gasped. Her body arched with the delicious shock of it. Her buttocks shook, and her legs splayed out wide. As she presented us again with the winking pink of her inner folds, the relaxation of her sphincter muscles also made the little tight orifice of her anus open to our inspection.

"Now, now my dear," the mayor said, "you know the rules. You must remain immobile if you don't want to be punished more." And with that he struck the girl again. Cut another dark furrow across the plump cheeks of her buttocks.

Again she cried out and moved.

Again the whip struck.

This time it cut a furrow exactly an inch above the welt it'd raised earlier. Marking thus, on the rounded plains of the girls welcoming ass, the field which it meant to plow, until the girl was sufficiently submissive to receive another plowing in her innermost centre.

Each time the girl cried out, her limbs strained against the inflicted pain and her head flew up, off the table top, as far as the graceful curve of her neck would permit, so that the flowing black ringlets of her locks would jump and then re-settle around her, like a veil.

The winking opening of her vulva, the relaxation of the tight little button of her ass, were telltale signs that the girl had done this thing many times before. They testified to the fact that she knew of the deeper pleasure that was yet to come, anticipated it, even as her plump behind was furrowed by the whip.

I could only imagine the further furrowing the mayor planned to inflict upon her once his arm tired of whipping her and he decided to make his full use of her open, ready orifices.

Again I remembered the tales I'd heard, and wondered how much use the girl had been subjected to prior to being tied up here, and by how many.

The thought of her body naked and splayed, everyone of its orifices filled by a man's cock, was unsettling, and I was thus quite unready for the voice that broke my thoughts.

"Seen enough?" Soames whispered at my side and I almost jumped.

So engrossed had I become in the spectacle of the young girl's exposed charms that I'd forgotten he was there with me.

"Come," he said, and taking hold of my sleeve he tugged me away from the two-way mirror and the revelations it held within its depths.

We moved on.

We stopped, but briefly, at the very next mirror. The room within was identically furnished with the one before, only this time there was no table.

Instead within the room was a man I didn't know. He was dressed in a short black robe of shiny stain with red, embossed symbols on it.

He lay on a mat on the floor. A white, blonde girl lay obscured and spread-eagled beneath him.

He was holding her arms stretched above her head.

The man's robe was open. And he'd positioned himself between the girl's spread legs. Her feet were drawn up. Knees splayed outwards, his buttocks rose and fell in rhythm with his grunts as he bore upon the girl with all the force of his weight.

We moved on.

Another mirror, another room beyond it.

This time we saw a brown woman on her hands and knees. Her full, ripe body was being enjoyed by two hulking men at the same time. Her face was buried deep into the middle of one of them. Her head was being restrained into that position by the powerful grip one of them exerted at the back of her neck. His meaty, thick hand was wrapped tightly into the black curls of her hair and he was pushing her face forward, towards him.

The other man was holding her tightly by the hips. Immobilised thus between the two men the brown woman could move neither forward nor backwards.

The man standing behind her had his hands hooked in her hips and he was charging her violently from behind. The full round moons of her buttocks shook with the force of each thrust from the man's hips. Her head buried deep into the other man's waist, she was making a choking muffled sound, halfway between a cry and a sob.

The two men were laughing.

"Stick it to her again," I heard one of them say to the other as we moved away and then a higher half-muffled cry followed by more ribald laughter.

Soames pulled me silently away and directed me towards the final mirror.

We came at last to stop before it.

I was shocked, numbed by the depravity of the licentious displays I'd witnessed this far, the suffering I believed these poor unfortunates were being subjected to. The fact that they also seemed to enjoy it did not make any easier the knowledge that their poor situation in life had conspired to place them in a position where their bodies had become the province of degenerates who wouldn't hesitate to perpetrate their innermost fantasy upon them.

But all this, was nothing to what I stood witness to at this last window.

The lights were low in the room beyond. In its centre was a low divan full of cushions and lying amongst them were two young brown girls of the sort I had come to recognise as being the mainstay of Soames' stable.

They seemed to form the staple of his flesh trade. And for good reason, I thought. For it was becoming apparent to me now, that many of these young girls were so happy to have escaped the desperation of their former lives that they cheerfully performed whatever service was asked of them in exchange.

The girls beyond the mirror this time were fully dressed, in clothes that hid all their loveliness. Their long hair had been bound and put up on top of their heads in a fashion that would not have looked out of place inside a church.

There was a man in the room, standing with his back to me.

As I peered into the gloom, I saw the man nod to the two girls and they languorously rose on their knees, facing each other in the middle of the bed. Their eyes not on each other, but upon the man standing facing them, they deftly unbuttoned, untied and unlaced each other's clothes.

I watched as bountiful breasts nippled in dusky peaks came into full view. The girls moved this way and that, shedding their clothes, running hands down the smooth plains of their bellies, touching themselves and each other.

All the while their eyes were upon the man.

"Undress me now," I heard him order them and I thought he must surely be one of those buyers I'd seen earlier bidding for female flesh, for his voice sounded vaguely familiar to me.

The girls complied, running to the man's side.

They removed his jacket first. Then his shirt and tie. And then, on their knees still, they undid the belt that held up his trousers. Working in concert they slid them down his chunky legs, slipped off his underpants.

One of the girls started licking the inside of the man's thigh. Her pointed, pink tongue ran up his leg from the knee, headed up towards an erection I could all too clearly imagine, but could not see, as his back was still presented to us.

The other girl stood up behind him and wrapped slim arms round his chest, pressing her full round breasts against his spine. She arched her back, pushing her hips forward and as she did so. Momentarily I admired the tight dimples of her full round buttocks, the lushness of her now unbound hair, the fullness of those breasts - and had circumstances been different, I would have gladly changed places with that man.

The first girl had reached her target now. Her face, framed by her long black hair, rose and fell as she sawed away at the man's erection, her lips working away at him as she endeavoured to pull as much of him as she could deep into her mouth.

Such was her skill that the man threw his head up towards the ceiling, his neck bending backwards at an almost painful angle...

He whipped an arm round behind his back. His hand played down the ridge of the second girl's spine and sought to cup and tightly squeeze the fullness of a round buttock, cruelly digging into her tender flesh as his passion peeked and the other girl's ministrations reached their height.

That's when, in the low light, I caught sight of the ring this man wore. It was of distinctive design. A round, gold ring with the symbol of a dove and a quill embossed upon it.

The symbol for freedom of the press!

And I felt the build up of moral dignity and outrage reach a new level inside me, and go past the point where I could control it. For I knew that ring well. I had seen it every time I discussed a story with my editor. I had heard the man lecture at length on its symbolism.

I opened my mouth to cry out. Unable to control myself any longer, feeling betrayed, confused, helpless in this new twist of Soames' elaborate trap and angry with the lustful betrayal of my own body.

Soames had outsmarted me right from the start. This destroyed my hope of ever beating him. He was probably enjoying some pleasure out of my desperation, not unlike that which he had so evidently enjoyed when he witnessed the usage those girls were being put to.

The pent up cry never reached my lips.

Soames' hand clapped itself across my mouth.

"Not now!" he hissed. "Let's talk. Later. But say nothing now."

And he led me away, a defeated man, bereft of all apparent hope. So much for all my plans, all my elaborate strategies. Head bowed, I let him guide me back past each two-way mirror, all windows to the dark depths of depravity residing in man's soul, to the place where we'd first entered.

Malakai awaited patiently for us there, the stolid expression firmly back on his face.

"Malakai will show you to your room," Soames explained. "I hope you can join me for dinner tonight. There's a lot we need to talk about."

His face was smiling as he said these words. It was even clearer to me now that he was enjoying to the full the effect his revelations had had upon my person. And thus it was as a broken man, dejected beyond all reasonable hope, that I followed Malakai's bulk, uncaring for what lay in store for me in the near future.

I flung myself down upon the narrow bed in my room in despair. It was the only other piece of furniture which graced the small quarters I'd been given.

Soames had given me a room which contrasted sharply with the plushness of those dens of sinful pleasure I had just so secretly observed. It reminded me of the exact nature of my station in his villa and further blackened my mood. It was lit by standing candles, great thick lumps of white wax that made the shadows flick about and played trick on tired eyes.

In the far corner, against the wall, was a simple table with a white linen tablecloth and upon it a plain bowl heavily laden with fruit.

Engrossed as I was in the blackness of my situation I neither saw nor heard Melissa enter.

The first I became aware of her presence was the heady smell of juniper and jasmine that was her own special brand. It so alarmed me that I jumped up from my narrow bed, certain that my imagination so inflamed by what I'd seen had sought its outlet into madness.

"It is me, Mr Lewis," she said.

And indeed it was so. By what secret magic were Melissa and the despicable Soames able to come and go as they pleased?

"The walls here have secret passages." Melissa answered my unasked question and I had time again to admire her unique beauty. The special cast of her delicate features. The almond shaped, slanted eyes and full lips.

She wore this time a tight grey tunic of some thin, clingy material and the contours of her voluptuous body were clearly visible underneath.

A brief image of that naked body came to me with a pained clarity. I experienced again the brief instant I had run my hands over the smooth lean back and cupped and squeezed her full round buttocks. I remembered the taste of her ripe breasts, the heat of her hardened nipples that had seared my lips, and I experienced once again that special shortening of breath, the tightening of my own arousal as it strained against the front of my trousers.

This time I fought it. It shamed me to remember the quick use I had made of her earlier, the ease with which I had descended into the same low depths Soames and his cronies wallowed in.

"What do you want?" I asked, and the effort to control my passions made my voice sound unnaturally hard.

If Melissa noticed she gave no indication. She stood where I'd first seen her in the room: in the corner, by the shadows. Head held low, downcast eyes, large and clear as crystal pools, only occasionally darting up to meet my own.

"I need your help, Mr Lewis," she pleaded, and once again I admired the exotic beauty of her form. "To escape from here. Away from my Master, away from Soames."

It was a cruel jest. I was in no position to help myself any more, let alone take the beautiful Melissa away from this monster in human form.

"I have no hope to offer," I said, and noticed how my words jerked her head up. The beautiful long neck, framed as it were by her long black hair added to the exquisiteness of her.

"Please!" She took a single step towards me and I couldn't help but notice how, as she moved from the shadows into the light, the tips of her exquisitely formed breasts were hard, pressed tightly against the thin fabric of her tunic, clearly outlined against it.

"Soames has the upper hand," I said. "There's little I can do. Even my own editor, a good man, of high principle, is in his thrall. He carouses on the young girls here, just like the rest."

It was sanctimonious of me, given my earlier debauched behaviour with Melissa. But earlier I'd thought I was at death's door, while now ... now I wasn't at all sure what was expected of me, or what would happen to me or my beloved friend Abu should Soames fail to convince me of the goodness of his works.

"Mr Lewis," Melissa's golden voice interrupted my thoughts, "all men are vulnerable. Trust not what you see here until you have found out for yourself. My master's power is both more and less than what it seems and he fears you more than you imagine."

I found that hard to believe myself but then if it gave me the pleasure to talk to Melissa, I thought, I could live even with such a lie.

"What exactly do you expect of me then?" I asked, trying to prolong my time with this beauty. Such was the corrupting influence of this place that even as I said the words my good intentions were already being betrayed and my mind was racing to find a way to close the gap, re-enact our earlier encounter. Her on her knees, in front of me, with my cock buried deep in her mouth. Me ready to go further with her.

Much further.

But just as I was about to attempt to once more taste the ripe offerings of this exotic creature I saw her tense and look alarmed.

"Someone's coming!"

A ruse, I thought -

There was a hard knock at the door, which I recognised as Malakai's iron hand, and then his voice: "Master Soames say you come to dinner."

"I'll be there in a few minutes," I said, my heart now thundering. How had Melissa been able to hear him come? I turned my head back to her, but there was nothing there.

Where Melissa had stood before now there was nothing. I took the last few steps and peered closely at the shadows, but found no doorway there.

Obviously the same superior engineering that made Soames' plush villa appear like a small summer house on the outside had been used to riddle the complex with secret passages and doors. One of them, at least, I thought with rising arousal, must lead to Melissa's bedroom.

I quickly checked my clothes, straightened my trousers and shirt and opened the door. The hulking form of Malakai instantly filled its frame.

I gave him no time to say anything smart. I stepped outside and said: "Lead the way then, my man, take me to the dining hall."

To my surprise I found that recent tension had done me good. I could at last think clearly again, and as I followed the silent brute I found myself again thinking of the mysterious Melissa, the strange dark look she'd cast towards me and the promise of unexpected enjoyment she so casually put my way.

For her, I thought, I wouldn't think twice before defying Soames completely.

3

The dining hall was massive and dark. The only light came from candles which cast fitful shadows this way and that, and a huge mahogany table of such opulence that I had seen only in films took up centre piece in it.

Soames sat at one end.

"Please, Frank, be seated."

I became aware that Malakai had somehow managed to vanish. The brute had withdrawn into the deepest shadows, and strain as I might I could see nothing of him in the poor light. "A meal should be an enchanting affair," Soames said. "Tonight we have a new serving wench, a fresh girl from one of the villages, and we have to help break her in."

He said these words quickly, not giving me much opportunity to consider what exactly was their import. Before I could reply Soames clapped his hands once and a door opened somewhere in the shadows to our left.

I wondered then, witnessing the ease with which this vile man exercised all his power, what exactly was his thrall over the beautiful Melissa. What was it that bound her so securely to him that she thought only I could help her escape?

In my mind's eye I saw again the wide scourge or lash as it must have snaked across Melissa's beautifully smooth chocolate coloured skin to make the marks I had seen, and I felt my loathing at this Englishman who now sat across from me.

But my curiosity was also aroused by his remarks.

"Our first course will be coconut soup," he said, interrupting my train of thoughts, "as refreshing and exotic as the young girl who will serve us."

Soames may have been guilty of many things but exaggeration was not one of them. Out of the shadows where a narrow doorway led to what I may only assume was the kitchen, came a willowy young form.

She was indeed, as Soames had said, refreshing and exotic. Her skin was smooth, seemingly flawless, and her delicate young face was framed by long dark hair tied back in a pony tail.

Immediately I recognised the girl as being one of the mulatto Indians, indigenous tribes of some of the more outflung villages that sprung up around Rio. In truth these villages were no more than glorified shanty towns, places where rape and incest went unchecked until some form of social order was imposed by a newly-formed gang.

In my work I had been to villages like these and I had seen the gangs at work. My articles had chronicled the violent manner in which this social order was imposed, the trade in flesh and drugs that subsequently financed the gangs and the inevitable slide into the mire that soon followed for the poor people unfortunate enough to have been trapped in their ruling area.

I had been reliably informed of one particular gang where its members where allowed to exercise complete power over all the girls in the village they ruled. Tales of girl-parties where twenty or thirty girls were kidnapped, held, and repeatedly raped by all the gang for two or three days before being released back into their families, were not uncommon in such situations.

The inevitable slide into prostitution that usually followed such gang-bangings had been one of the facts revealed by my investigations, and though I had not been able to unearth sufficient material for a complete article, I had at the time, been very intrigued by the type of experiences these girls would later have.

So it was with renewed interest, my thoughts about Melissa and Soames momentarily forgotten, that I watched this young girl's progress towards us.

As she came into the light thrown by the bigger candles nearest us I could admire her at leisure. Exotic indeed. She was dressed in casual peasant garb. A wide skirt that was held at her willowy waist by a brown leather belt and, as it dropped past her knees, emphasised the swing of her wide hips. She wore a loose blouse closed all the way to the neck, and the suggestive bounce of her breasts as she walked towards us hinted of a bounty that would have driven any man mad with lust.

"She speaks no English," Soames informed me as the girl came to stand beside him.

I could now see her more clearly. Her fine chocolate burnished skin was tinged with a darker colour which I took to be a sign of her shame for the current situation she found herself in. Her eyes, large and clear as pools, were downcast. Submissive.

Unconsciously I found myself comparing this fresh, young beauty to Melissa's fine features. Although this girl was not as alluring, I had to admit that there was a freshness and reticence about her that I was finding enchanting.

With a nod Soames beckoned for the girl to serve him. Not meeting his eye still, she put the pot of soup she was carrying by the handles on the table and ladled a generous measure into the fine china bowl in front of her white master.

As she was doing that Soames, with his hand, drew my attention to the fact that the girl was barefoot. Her feet, small and delicate like a child's, had stubby little toes that ended nails that were painted a vivid red.

"Where she comes from they have no shoes," Soames said as his hand brushed the shapely calf of the girl, as she bent across from him to measure out a second ladleful. The bottom of her long skirt stopped at mid-calf and Soames now drew my attention to the shapeliness of her ankles.

"You can tell a lot by a young girl's ankles, of course," he said. "Like the finest horses, women's ankles reveal a lot about their bloodlines, the potential they hide. You can get large ankles for example, big-boned joints that mar the symmetry of a woman's legs. They mark strong women, simple but hard-working, capable of being trained to service ten or twenty men a night."

He winked as he said this, his eyes carefully on mine.

I was mesmerised by the weaving motion of his hand, the way it moved around the girl's ankle, up along the gentle curve of her calf, down again to illustrate Soames' point.

"There are women with hardly any ankle at all. Peasant girls of sturdy design, with legs that end straight down. They can be put to hard labour, both manual and sexual, without showing any ill-effects. Some of our less sophisticated clients prefer such women. They exhibit none of the finesse of our better trained girls but they are grateful for anything you are willing to give them. They know their station in life and they are willing to do anything to please."

He stopped explaining and motioned for the girl to serve me.

She complied immediately, eyes still downcast. The pot of soup was in front of her chest, just below the level of her breasts which bounced as she walked like they had a life of their own.

She came to stand by my side and as she put the soup down and reached across with her ladle to fill my own bowl, I smelled the fragrance of her body, and was captivated by the fine bones of her ankles and what little was visible of her legs.

I felt then this burning desire to emulate Soames' example, to reach out and cup the delicate ankle bones, to feel the burnished smoothness of this girl's skin. It was, I thought, this English devil's influence, placing such tempting morsels within such easy reach. He was trying to rouse the beast in me, which since my brief encounter with Melissa, I was just beginning to recognise.

I resisted.

The girl finished serving me and waited patiently by my side until at a nod from Soames she was given permission to move away again.

Following Soames' example I tasted the soup. It was indeed delicious, flavoursome beyond expectation.

"Then," Soames continued as we ate, "there are girls like this fresh wench here, delicate ankles, finely shaped legs, bodies which hide hidden fires that need only to be uncovered and carefully fanned before they leap into flame." He grinned wickedly at me and my indignation now sprang to the front and gave me voice.

"But surely you just mean to use them and abuse them. You will sell this girl into sexual slavery, a life of servitude, where God knows what vileness she will have to withstand until her beauty and desirability give out."

Soames stopped eating and looked up at me. "Is that what you really think?"

"I've seen how gangs work," I said. "I've been there first hand. These poor unfortunates have no say in anything. Their lowly station in life has conspired to rob them of any possible choice."

"I don't work that way though," he said.

"But you will sell her."

"Yes, indeed. Pleasure is what my operations are always about, Frank. Our buyers come from as wide afield as San

Francisco, or rich Mexicans who want to purchase themselves beautiful servants, docile wives. Oh yes, selling is what we do here."

"So how are you different?" I challenged him.

"For a start, I give these unfortunates a real choice. Their families are well rewarded for the girls' indenture to me. It is their first and only real chance to escape the poverty of the slums they live in. The girls themselves are then trained. Our clients are carefully vetted. We don't cater to men who simply want a mere sex-slave."

"No?"

"No. Did you learn nothing from our little tour backstage? The gentlemen who come to us come with something specific in mind. Sex itself, simple sex is such a vicarious thing to seek. Pleasure, on the other hand has deeper depths. There is the double edge of pain and denial to enhance its appeal. The fine mixture of all three which makes any sexual experience, any at all, well worth having. That's what we're all about here Frank, sex as an art."

He clapped his hands again, stopping any reply, and I watched the girl approach us, wondering if she knew what was in store for her. Soames' talk not withstanding, the man was into the business of buying these young unfortunates from large poor families who could hardly afford to feed themselves, and then selling them at auctions like the one Abu had brought me to.

The thought of my boyhood friend momentarily sidetracked me, but only momentarily, for now the girl was in full view, bending across Soames to put a fresh plate on the table in front of him, and as she did so the hem of her wide peasant skirt drew higher up the backs of her calves, reaching almost to the backs of her knees.

In silent fascination, tinged now with a hint of envy, I watched as Soames casually put his hand on the back of the girl's left calf, and slowly moved it up and down her leg, initially savouring the gentle curve of her calf, the freshness of her smooth skin.

Then the hand began to move higher up the back of the girl's leg...

All this time she continued with her duties, piling fresh food onto Soames' plate, her eyes staying submissively downcast. Her fresh innocent face was totally blank, as if she'd resigned herself to taking everything that happened to her as her due in this world.

I watched Soames' hand move higher and higher until it disappeared completely up the girl's leg, its progress barely visible beneath the fabric of her skirt. Its movements were completely hidden, but its effects were not.

A deeper flush of what I could only construe to be shame stained the smooth skin of the girl's face, and while her hands moved still, serving Soames, her teeth, small and porcelain white, now bit down on her lower lip, to stop her making any sound.

Soames had his hand high up the girl's skirt now and I could only imagine the vulnerable softness of her soft round buttocks, the untouched smoothness of her flesh, which he now so casually manhandled.

The hand did something and I saw the girl's body stiffen momentarily. Her small even teeth bit down even harder, leaving small indentations to mar the perfection of her lower lip.

Then Soames removed his hand and motioned for the girl to serve me next.

She approached me timidly, walking warily on dainty feet probably expecting similar treatment.

I let her serve my food, staring defiantly at Soames the whole while. Instead of taking offence at my refusal to follow his example, to experience and taste the temptation he so casually offered me, he seemed to take pleasure from viewing my distaste.

"Very touching, Frank," he said the moment the girl had completed her task and after a signal from him, walked away from us, "and totally meaningless. If you think you're doing the girl a favour, think again. You said yourself you've been to the villages, seen the gangs' work first-hand. What is it they lead these girls to? Prostitution, drugs, crime. They gang-bang them whenever they feel like it and the rest of the time they're content to let them live a life spent in squalor."

Though what he was he was saying was true, the duplicity of his stance was too much for me and after a few moments I could contain myself no longer. "And you're a philanthropist I suppose?" I asked. "You offer them better?"

"I offer them a life spent in comfort and safety, exercising options they are eminently suited for. Even our most often used girls are looked after better, with careful medical supervision, than the best possible life these unfortunates can ever aspire to."

I wasn't convinced, but convincing me now, I realised, was the furthest thing from the Englishman's mind as he motioned once more for the remnants of our meal to be cleared away.

Once again the girl stepped out from the shadows. As if sensing what was in store for her she worked quickly, with delicate features firmly set, a stoic look on her face.
I watched her retreat back into the shadows and come back, this time empty-handed.

"Desert," Soames murmured, without explaining any further. An intense expression had crept over his face and I watched now intrigued.

The girl stood silently before us. The magic allure of her face and form, hidden as it was by her buggy clothing was nonetheless enhanced by the candlelight, and Soames let her wait a awhile longer, studying her in silence. Then, with a click of his fingers he motioned to her to approach him, and silently motioned at the belt that held her peasant skirt up.

The girl hesitated. Then her hands went to the wide leather belt at her willowy waist and pulled at the buckle. The belt was tight and the girl's fingers trembled, but she finally managed to get the cusp undone and take the belt off.

It must have been the only thing holding her skirt up, because the minute the belt was off, her skirt dropped to the floor, and pooled round her ankles, lying there like a banner.

Her blouse underneath was long. It came almost to midthigh. But standing like that, with her shapely legs revealed, the coarse peasant skirt pooled round her ankles in defeat, she presented a most alluring sight.

"What do you think Frank?"

Soames seemed to be entranced with the magic attraction of the moment every bit as I was.

Caught as I was in my own inner struggle I didn't reply. One part of me, the rational part, was telling me that this was all a madness. I had no right to be there. I had come to do a job, to uncover Soames' sex-trade. And now, captive though I was, I should be planning on how to best affect my escape. The other part of me, the dark part that resides within the breast of each and everyone of us, was now fixated by the girl. This part told me that yes, though captive, there would be no harm in at least tasting a little of the forbidden fruit on offer here. Nothing could be gained by my being recalcitrant and by appearing to capitulate I might even find a weakness in Soames that would then enable me to defeat him.

I sat spellbound, admiring the fullness of the girl's young thighs, the way her legs filled out, touching almost all the way to the part where the tail of the blouse hid them from view. I imagined those legs opening wide, being spread to receive a man, and I admit I felt desire, like no other time before.

I understood now the great urge some men feel to despoil young virgins. It was, I suppose, akin to treading on virgin snow. Leaving your mark behind for posterity, however ephemeral. Being the first one to get there.

Furtively, I dropped my hand beneath the level of the table and massaged the ache in my groin.

"The top now," Soames whispered.

Slowly her fingers unbuttoned the row of buttons of her blouse. One by one. I was given a momentary flash of burnished flesh, the proud swelling of young, untasted breasts. Then the flaps fell together again, hiding them from view.

For long moments Soames and I sat there silently, savouring the sight of the girl's body. We could clearly see the rapid rise and fall of her breasts. They way they pushed the open blouse out. Where the unbuttoned blouse parted, I could see a low-cut bra of simple white cotton, round orbs the colour of milk chocolate overflowing its cups.

"Let's see some more," Soames said to me, and he motioned for the girl to remove her blouse completely.

Moving slowly, revealing one shoulder at a time, with a natural if unpractised ease, the girl shrugged out of it completely.

Her beauty was finally revealed.

She had on a cheap white cotton bra, low cut and far too small for her. The colour of the garment contrasted with her chocolate coloured skin most effectively, setting off her beauty without much effort. Her breasts were full, round, heavy with ripeness and strong with youth, barely restrained by the cheap garment. The smooth flatness of her stomach gave way to an almost imperceptible rise that led naturally into the curve of her belly and the junction between her legs.

Through the sheer white cotton underpants I could clearly see the outline of the plump lips of her sex.

Her hips were wide enough to entice a man, but not yet stretched by childbirth. They gave way to the fullness of her round thighs, the tapering legs and delicate ankles. The girl was indeed a beauty, not in the same class as Melissa, I could now truthfully attest to, but a beauty nevertheless.

"The bra," Soames said, snapping his fingers.

She moved first one strap off one shoulder, then the other, before putting both arms behind her back, to undo the garment. The movement made the taut mounds of her breasts press against the white cotton fabric, and her nipples were clearly outlined for our eyes to feast upon.

In resignation, she let the simple white bra fall to the growing pool of fabric round her feet.

Her flesh revealed was every bit as magnificent as it had been hinted at. In the candlelight her breasts heaved with every breath she took. Their dark, round nipples, large full moons set in the centre of smooth milk-chocolate coloured mounds were erect with fear.

Soames snapped his fingers again, his gesture unmistakable.

The girl's delicate hands went to her waist. There was a moment's hesitation, then she bent down, breasts momentarily pointing at the floor as she pushed her plain white panties down her thighs, past her knees, almost to her ankles, and timidly stepped out of them.

"Straighten up!" The girl must have understood by the tone.

Shyly at first, then defiantly, as if taking pride in her undeniable beauty, she stood up straight, threw her shoulders back so that her breasts rode higher and levelled her gaze over our heads.

To my shame, I felt my member respond at the sight of her unused nakedness.

Where her shapely thighs met, the girl's fuzz was dark,

bushy. Thick, tight curls hid her sex from our view.

She was indeed a beauty and, deep down, I began to realise more fully the attraction of Soames' auctions to the rich men who frequented them.

We sat there in silence, admiring the play of light and shadow on the exposed plains of the girl's body. A body that would soon, I thought, be the plaything of some rich buyer, to be used for his exclusive pleasure, and despite my earlier thoughts of righteousness and my best intentions, the more beastly side of me betrayed me once more and I found myself lusting after the disrobed young unfortunate who now stood trembling before us.

Without a word Soames stood up. He had shed his jacket, and was in shirt sleeves and tieless as he walked towards the girl. There was no mistaking the large bulge in front of his riding trousers.

I recalled his words about training the girl, and I realised with horror tinged with a degree of glee that I was about to witness exactly what Soames had meant by those words. Now he undid the front of his trousers to reveal his full erection. The sight of the throbbing thickness of his member would normally have been enough to have me on my feet in disgust, ready to do anything to prevent the girl from meeting a fate that would by any measure be both premature and cruel, but the darker part of myself now prevailed.

I watched in rapt silence as Soames approached the naked, trembling girl as she crossed a protective arm across her heaving bosom. Her left hand spread protective fingers over the tightly curled fuzz nestling between her tender thighs.

Soames ignored this reaction.

He snapped his fingers once more and out of the deep shadows behind the girl, appeared the monstrous Malakai.

"Tie her!"

With an evil grin on his face that reminded me of the

man's public performance with Melissa, the hulking brute seized the young girl's arms by the elbows and with a length of thick twine, roughly tied her hands together behind her back. He pulled them tautly behind her, making the proud mounds of her breasts rise even higher. The dark round nipples, hardened with fear, and now pain, lanced the air in front of us.

Soames waited silently, erect penis exposed, almost an imitation of those lusty statues of Pan I'd once seen on a trip to a Greek museum.

His task finished, Malakai withdrew back into the shadows. This time though, my eyes accustomed as they'd become to the flickering candlelight, I was able to see the shape of the man leaning against the far wall.

Soames now advanced towards the girl. Indifferent to the silent plea so easy to see in her big brown eyes, he reached out with one hand and experimentally cupped the plentiful mound of her left breast. His hands squeezed and kneaded the chocolate coloured flesh, savouring its fine texture.

"What do you say Frank? Not bad, hey?"

He rubbed his thumb roughly over the girl's nipple, and then trapping the tumescent flesh between thumb and forefinger he tweaked it painfully, rolling it roughly at the same time.

Beads of sweat broke the hairline at the girl's brow and her lower lip trembled as she struggled not to cry out.

"One of the finer specimens my men have been able to find," Soames informed me over his shoulder as he let go of the girl's proud breast and dropped his hand down her front, the tip of his penis touching her middle, just above the navel, as he leaned towards her.

Like a white mamba the Englishman's thin arm snaked over the smooth plain of the girl's belly, down the gentle curve of her body, and with a lunge fasted itself cruelly upon the mound of her sex.

The girl shuddered, rocked. Bent forward almost. Her full breasts shook and bounced. Her eyes pleaded silently with him, and her even white teeth bit down upon her lips.

"Hot little minx, isn't she?" remarked Soames coolly.

His hand, nestled tightly between the young girl's tender thighs, moved this way and that, and his long index finger sought quick entry into her body.

"A virgin!'" he exclaimed in surprise. "Pity! We could have used her first ourselves a little, but it would spoil her value."

He withdrew his hand with a slow, rubbing motion, drawing the fingers slowly through the tightly nestled curls. "That will have to go of course," he said conversationally to me, indicating the girl's tightly curled pubes. "No sense in hiding that light under a bushel!"

Having thus debased the girl, he walked slowly around her, eyeing her up now with the experienced buyer's eye. He hefted a pear-shaped buttock, chuckling appreciatively to himself.

"Nice ass," he said, rubbing his erect penis against her hip as he itemised her for my benefit.

"Fertile hips, the sort you want spread beneath you," he said, as he drew my attention to the curve of the girls' hips, the full line of her thighs and the tight rise of the mounds of her ass. "Just the kind of thing to make a buyer reach for his wallet. The instant they see this ass" - he playfully stroked the curve of the girl's round ass again, then slapped her buttocks - "they'll think of nothing more than ploughing these little mounds from behind. Storming the fort while hanging onto these" - another playful slap delivered at her breasts this time, making them jump and bounce. "You see how money's made then Frank?"

He came to stop directly in front of the girl, but half-turned towards me.

"You disgust me," I spat out, but my voice was tight with suppressed lust.

"A little butt-fucking, a little breast-fucking and then ploughing the deeper valleys," Soames said with a wide grin. "That's what life's all about, Frank. But the best value, as I told you, comes with the spice of the mix. Pleasure and pain. That's what holds the edge of delight."

And with those words he slapped the girl again. His open palm hit her hard across the face, making her locks bounce on her shoulders.

The girl was so shocked with the unexpected blow she opened her mouth to scream, and then Soames hit her again. This time the other way. Where his hand had made impact with her flesh, the skin had taken a darker hue further adding to the overall allure of the girl's condition.

Before she could recover enough to react again, Soames took a rope of the girl's hair in one hand, and, tugging it violently, forced her on her knees in front of him.

The girl cried out as her knees hit the cold, hard floor. Her breasts bounced with the movement. Her thighs fell apart, offering tantalising hints of the secret treasure they guarded at her very centre.

The girl's head was now level with the Englishman's bared middle, his throbbing penis in direct line with her lips. Tightening his hold upon her hair, he tugged even harder and as the girl's mouth instinctively opened for her to cry out once more he thrust his hips violently forward.

The bulbous tip of his erect member, engorged with lust as it was, penetrated the round oval of the girl's soft mouth, gagging her completely and smothering her pained gasp. I heard her gulp as she struggled to accommodate the entire length of him in her mouth.

"Come here, Frank." Soames' voice was tight with excitement. His hips pistoned back and forth, his hand holding the girl's head pressed tightly against his groin, preventing her from pulling away. I could hear the gulping sounds she was making as she performed what Soames was forcing her to do.

My eyes were drawn to the erect dancing tips of her full breasts that rubbed against Soames' thighs as his penis slid in and out of the warm cavity of her mouth.

"Feel her ass," Soames bid me and caught in the daze of the moment, I complied.

The girl's body was really a work of art. Unschooled as she obviously was in the ways of sex, she nonetheless took Soames' erection deep in her mouth, sucked it in as much as she could, controlling the gag reflex and then pulled back again. Saliva ran down the sides of her mouth to coat her chin, her lips a ripe red ring round Soames' cock.

I walked up behind her. The sight of her tied hands, her very helplessness, the muffled noises she was making, transformed the darkness that hides deep in the breast of every man and gave it shape and form that soon took me completely over. I became aware of the pounding sound of my heartbeat, the rush of blood, loud in my ears, even as my eyes were drawn as Soames intended to the exposed sort round curves of the girl's ass.

Positioning myself directly behind her, I hesitated for an instant.

I could see the top of the girl's bobbing head. I could see where her full lips strained to encompass the girth of Soames' penis.

Her eyes, I imagined by her reactions, reflected a mixture of fear and pleasure.

Tentatively almost, I put my hands upon her shoulders. Felt the searing heat of her flesh. I pushed her bodily forward, unbalancing her, so that her head was suddenly buried in Soames middle, her face pressed against the base of his cock and the muffled sucking sounds she was making instantly became deeper, choked by the length of cockmeat she had to suck.

My hands roamed over her shoulders.

If the flesh of the usherettes I had touched earlier that night had been smooth and pampered, this girl's flesh felt fresh, as yet untasted, undergoing its very first transformation as the heat of passion rose to tinge it.

"Do it!" Soames hissed, his mad eyes upon me, the chords standing out thickly on either side of his neck as the girl's efforts reached their height.

It wasn't fear of him, nor any sense of obedience that guided my hands as I slid them down the girl's shoulders, onto her chest. My palms found the fullness of her breasts and my hands cupped the proud mounds. I savoured their texture and feel, much as Soames had done moments earlier.

I squeezed them. Pushed them together. Kneaded her pliant flesh with growing excitement.

"Her ass!" Soames gasped above me. "Grab her ass!"

And, deep in the hold of my own personal brand of madness, I obeyed.

I let go of the girl's young breasts. Slid both hands down her back, then beneath her buttocks. The full plumpness of her ass pushed me further into the crazy darkness that ate at my sense of right and wrong, and that's when I lost control.

My fingers dug and squeezed into her pliant flesh. I half lifted her, tilting her forward again, so suddenly that she almost gagged on Soames' cock as the tip of it slid deep into her mouth, touched the very back of her throat.

My hands sought and found the softness of the inner sides of her thighs, where her legs joined her ass, and I squeezed and kneaded once more, gasping for breath, feeling my own unspent passion rise and being unaware of it.

The tight curve of the girl's plump cheeks guided my hands. My index fingers found the open cleft of her sex, even as my hands squeezed her flesh, and unhesitatingly dived in. She was wet. Hot to the touch.

I slid my index finger into her, to the limit of the little shield. Her juices flowed freely out of her to run down my wrist and I could only imagine the intimate pleasure to be experienced if I replaced my finger with the risen part of my male anatomy.

With my free hand I sought out the fullness of her ripe breasts again and I sunk my hands into their softness. My fingers teased out her nipples, pinching them and rolling the hardened tips, while my index finger pistoned in and out of her hot, tight cunt.

That, and the combination of having Soames' entire length buried deep in her throat, was too much for the poor unfortunate.

The instant I plunged the very tip of a second finger into the hot wet depths of her, she let out a choked cry. Soames above her echoed that. He cried out and his body stiffened and I heard the girl gulp and lap as she struggled to swallow the splashes of semen he was pouring into her mouth.

Only I was yet unfulfilled.

"Enough - let her go," Soames ordered above me, and with a soft plopping sound he withdrew from the girl's avid mouth.

His cock, I saw, was now limp.

The instant he drew back, the girl fell forward, legs folded still beneath her, knees splayed, head down, touching the cold floor. Her dark cascade of hair hid her face from us. Only her heaving back told me of the sobs that now wracked her body.

The still present ringing of mad desire in my ears made me ignore her state, and my eyes were drawn like magnets to the inviting darkness between her legs.

As she had fallen forward like that, her thighs, touching all the way behind, parted a little at that special place as they neared her tight ass, to reveal the slit of her pink sex, a perfectly round drop of moisture glistening like a secret pearl inside.

I licked my lips in anticipation and made to edge towards her.

"Let her be!" Soames said.

He had straightened his clothes by now and was busy pouring himself a glass of dark red wine. "She's useless to us unless she is trained, Frank, useless."

Reluctantly I rose to my feet, uncertain yet of what I felt, what I'd done...

"But though she must remain untouched, so that her value can hold," Soames continued, offering me a goblet of red wine, "she must be taught the pleasure that comes with pain."

He motioned then to Malakai who had been watching all this, eagerly been awaiting just this moment, from the shadows.

"I want her prepared well," he said, "for next week's bazaar."

Malakai nodded at once.

Soames took my arm and gently guided me towards the door. "Come Frank, it is over for the night," he said. The enmity that had been in his manner earlier was now entirely gone.

I looked over my shoulder and caught a glimpse of Malakai dragging the girl roughly by her tied arms, pushing her face down upon the long table. Tied like this, she was helpless as a rag doll in the man's massive grip. And I suspected there was nothing gentle in Malakai's love-making technique.

I was given a brief glimpse of the girl's vulnerable ass, exposed and unprotected in the candlelight, and then

Malakai's huge bulk obscured everything as he shed his voluminous trousers and reared up behind her.

But I still heard the agonised cries of the girl as he repeatedly sodomised her, preserving the purity of her cunt, preparing her well no doubt for the sex show she was to perform at the coming bazaar Soames had mentioned.

4

Soames did not leave me much time to recover.

My blood still boiling, the memory of the girl's warm pliant flesh in my hands still fresh, her agonised cries as Malakai schooled her still ringing in my ears, I let myself be led back to my room.

Frustrated, unfulfilled, and securely in the grip of my own dark demon, my passion for Melissa and my anger at Soames now riding high.

"Goodnight," he said, "count this as your first night with us, Frank. Only two more to go,"

I should have said something to the devil. I would have indeed had not his strange dark red wine so much further addled my senses, that in my current state I could not trust myself to say anything meaningful.

The door closed behind me with a final thud and I was for once grateful for the peace and quiet my secluded room, indeed my prison, now afforded me.

But I was deceived.

There was the trace of a familiar perfume lingering in the air of my room. The smell of jasmine that was Melissa! I looked around hoping to see her, but the lingering perfume was the only trace of her presence - yet beside the pillow on my bed reposed a mask of black velvet!

It was trepidation as much as lust that made my heart beat wildly. The thought of Melissa, her exotic beauty, the soft resilience of her flesh that only hours ago I had so carelessly tasted, renewed the flames of lust aroused by Soames' young serving girl.

Next to the mask, upon the pillow, was a small note in thin rice paper. A woman's elaborate script upon it had written simply: PUT IT ON.

I stood indecisively by the bed.

Put it on?

A mask?

Whatever Soames might have said, whatever he might have wanted, it was clear to me now that there was more than one plan being put to use here.

I was almost convinced that Melissa wanted to be rid of the foul Englishman. Her exotic beauty was ripe for bestowing upon a new master. And that new master could easily be me... to feel Melissa writhe spread-eagled beneath my bulk, to have her pleasure me in every way, every night, whenever I wanted...

Against my own wish almost, I felt the burgeoning tip of my cock press itself against the cotton fabric of my thin trousers. The frustration within me was manifesting itself in a burning ache deep inside my cock and I thought, tonight, nothing would be better than Melissa to relieve this ache.

In truth, I'd temporarily shed all my principles, and longed for nothing more than to bury my cock deep in some girl's soft, warm body. To have her suck the semen out of me. To hear her cry out as I rammed my cock up her ass, stretched the folds of her tight button before sinking my sword again into the welcoming wetness of her cunt.

Wrapped within these fevered thoughts, it took a few moments longer for me to become aware of yet another change in my room.

In the far corner, where the table that held the wines reposed, an unknown hand had drawn an arrow in red upon the white tablecloth, an arrow that pointed directly at a blank spot upon the wall.

I picked up the rice paper, crumpled it and put it deep in one pocket of my black trousers.

Then I picked up the mask.

Melissa had said that Soames' place was full of doors.

I walked over to the table. The arrow was all the keys I needed.

I put on the soft velvet mask and then explored the wall at the very spot where the arrow pointed. For long moments nothing happened, then there was a click, barely audible, and an entire section of the wall slid silently back.

I took one deep breath, aware now that I was poised on the brink. Here I was, caught in the grip of sexual need, my lust needing to be satisfied and the unknown lying promising God knows what ahead. Never daring to think too analytically in case my courage betrayed me, I stepped through the opening that had become revealed.

The artfully concealed doorway slid shut behind me the instant I was through it, and I found myself in almost total darkness. There were unfamiliar smells in the air and barely audible sounds which I could not yet make out.

I fancied I found myself in a newly-formed kind of hell. The sort of place Soames would be expected to reign supreme over. Patiently I waited for my eyes to adjust to the poor light. There was a long, narrow corridor. Doubtless another of Soames' famous passages that riddled his villa of perversion like a honeycomb.

My heart was beating faster in anticipation. The recent training of Soames' newly acquired servant had left me feeling on a strange edge and there was a battle going on within my breast. All my intellect, all my civilised training cried out for action against Soames. I had to do something to expose the terrible trade in female flesh he had started. But there was also a part of me that agreed that by and large a great many of the unfortunates he ensnared in his terrible net achieved a fate by far superior to anything they had a right to expect when in the bosoms of their natural families.

My journalistic career had taken me far enough into these poverty-stricken societies to acquaint me handsomely with the daily terrors they all had to endure. Hunger, prostitution, incest, regular beatings, drugs, rape and young deaths was their common lot in life, and more often than not I had seen such fate administered to them at the hands of their families as much as by the members of the various gangs that soon took over their neighbourhoods and villages.

It was a lot which they suffered in a stoic silence, for their illiteracy allowed them no other means of bearing up to what many an educated woman would consider an intolerable fate.

So, it is with these mixed feelings warring inside my head and a ravenous sex-crazed beast unleashed in my breast that I cautiously advanced down this semi-dark tunnel, every sense on the alert, a modern-day Orpheus willingly descending into a new kind of Hades in search of - I knew not what.

The back of my mind was full of imagery I had yet to deal with. The suppressed cries of newly awakened passion, the muffled half-choked sobs of Soames' new girl as she sucked upon her master's penis, and her pained cries as Malakai brutally thrust himself upon her, cruelly sodomising her. All this, set off against a backdrop where Melissa had taken centre-stage in my own private fantasies. Momentarily, in the darkness, I fancied I smelled her special scent again, and almost convinced myself that this was in truth a secret assignation, that Melissa had left me the signs that would take me to her night chamber where I would truly discover, once and for all, the real meaning of Paradise.

Vividly I recalled again the special taste of the smooth skin of her bountiful, ripe breasts, the hardening nipple flesh as my tongue savagely teased them, the fullness of the round moons of her ass as I dug my fingers into them.

It was in this excited state that I took the final few steps down the end of the narrow corridor and pushing against a white coloured panel set against the dark wood of the wall, entered at last into a universe of lust.

Do not think that I am exaggerating here!

Up to that moment I was still Frank Lewis, the renowned investigative journalist. I may not have been whiter than white but I had been no rake either. My experience of the world had been one where the strong preyed on the weak. Where sex, most often, was just another means of exercising power. Where men's minds devised new and potent forms of debasement for their women.

In that world I knew exactly where I stood.

My sexual experiences had been such that I had learnt that women were not above using their beauty as a weapon. Their charms as bargaining points. Whatever may be said for or against my view of things, it at least enabled me to function. To lead a life with some purpose, a sense of meaning, no matter how ill-defined.

But the large chamber I stood in after I pushed the panel aside ushered me into a world that I had been taught was extinct, gone three thousand years before with the fall of the Roman empire.

The chamber I was in, for no other word will adequately describe the dimensions of the huge room I had entered, was full of masked men. Yes, all of them wore masks like mine. These masks hid the face and mouth, left an opening for the nostrils, and hooded the eyes so that only the pupils were visible.

There must have been a hundred men at least. Some were

dressed in clothes not unlike my own. Others wore loose shirts that came to about mid-thigh. A few wore barely anything at all, their big hairy bellies forming a bulge just over the swollen tips of their dicks.

Everywhere I looked I saw male erections in various states of arousal.

The air smelled of excitement.

There was an underlying drumbeat coming from somewhere and it was underscored by suppressed grunts and moans and female screams of passion.

Amongst these hundred-odd men were just as many women.

The women were all brown. Some dark as midnight, with the tightly ringed cascading hair of the lower-city castes, others half-breeds of varying shades of chocolate. Some were almost white.

Most were bound.

As I watched, I saw one woman being roughly tied up by three men. There was a metal frame they stood her up in. Her arms and feet were shackled by black leather ringlets, attached to chains, and as I watched one of the men pulled the chains tight, so that the woman's naked body was spread-eagled in the imitation of a star.

She was completely naked, with small pert breasts, the nipples erect and proudly lancing the air in front of her. Her mons, I saw, had been completely shaved, giving everyone an intimate view of her clit as her feet were most roughly pushed apart, the shackles placed there by one of the kneeling men.

The other two were busy finishing off the tying on each of her wrists, until stretched out taut as she was, like a starfish, she stood unable to make a move to cover her body or protect herself.

The men took up positions around her, quietly deciding

amongst themselves the order in which they were to use her. The one who'd tied her feet up produced a long black dildo, wickedly curved and horny tipped. The raised studs on its latex surface gleamed wickedly even from where I stood. He proceeded to push it into the woman's mouth, completely gagging her, and her eyes widened in pained surprise.

Fascinated, I watched as her lips struggled to wrap themselves around the thick circumference of the dildo. Her throat muscles relaxed to take it deep down her larynx. She opened her mouth wider to enable herself to breathe.

At the same time, one of the other two men approached the woman from behind and pressed himself violently against her. He was dressed in a billowing cloak of red and black and it hid from me most of what he was doing.

The way his hands clawed frantically at the woman's hips, though, the way her tautly stretched body swayed with rhythmic motion and the manner in which her already wide eyes strove to widen even further, were testimony to the fact that a deep invasion of her body was being perpetrated before my eyes. That the man, in fact, was busying himself with fucking her up the ass, stretching her tight orifice with every thundering stroke.

The third man now positioned himself.

He squeezed expertly in beside the man who was busy shoving the thick black dildo in and out of the woman's mouth, opened up his trousers to let his erect penis come free, and, seizing the woman roughly by the thighs, he bent his knees and took careful aim at her cunt.

The positioning of the woman's tied legs had pulled the lips of her sex apart, so that it was displayed in all its glory, inviting whatever use the man intended to put it to as he took careful aim, aligning the thick bulbous head of his erect penis with the shaved slit of his victim's sex. He hesitated moments longer, whether teasing the woman or prolonging the expectation of pleasure he was about to receive I couldn't say.

Then, with a violent thrust of his knees, he straightened up. His shaft invaded the woman's body. Being used already by the other two men, this new invasion of her body made the woman cry out, a long half-choked cry that made the three men using her redouble their efforts. I saw her body vibrate back and forth, the fullness of her buttocks being flattened by repeated thrusts, her lips bulging around the dildo being shoved back and forth, while her shaved pussy, its puckered, hairless lips engulfing the pumping prick of the third man, glistened with her secretions.

The juices of the man's rough taking of her gave her cunt a glistening look that I realised probably meant that even after the three men had had their fill and were finished with her, this woman would be left tied-up and vulnerable, warmed-up as it were and ready for the attention of many a male to come.

There were many men of my acquaintance who thought that a well-used woman was warmed-up enough for further joy, and even if her pussy was too swollen and red from too much loving to suit their particular requirements there would be other orifices to receive their attention and satisfy their urgent needs.

I left the three men to their pleasure and pushed through the crowd in a semi-daze.

Assaulted as I was by a hundred arousing sights and sounds, my heart pumped wildly, for what was I to make out of the blatant display of such carnal pleasures? How was I to react, already aroused as I was in my frustrated state, to the sight of naked women, their bodies totally hairless, being made to bend this way and that while men lined up to take their pleasure of them?

Unconsciously, my steps took me past many such sights

until I stopped and looked. I saw that I had arrived at a secluded spot where no other male stood just now. In one corner, in front of me there was a row of low beds. They had thin mattresses and they were raised on low iron legs, barely off the floor.

Upon the beds lay young brown girls, the tight flesh of their naked bodies and the overall slimness of their flesh marking them as being younger than the others. They were all blindfolded and gagged, and they'd been tied spread-eagled upon the iron beds.

"Come on," I heard someone say to me, even as I looked mesmerised upon the sight presented by the girls' open legs, secured in as wide a position as possible.

I turned to see another masked man standing beside me. "You must be new," he said matter-of-factly. "These are all virgins. Guaranteed. We have the pleasure of breaking them in."

He motioned for me to follow and, caught in a trancelike mood, I did so.

My newly acquired friend took me by the elbow to hurry me up and shouldering his way past a group of men who had surrounded a naked woman on her hands and knees, took me to the row of beds. There were six altogether, and the girls upon them were exquisite.

Three of them I saw, had been tied on their backs.

Their arms, stretched tautly above their heads, prevented them from any movement, and their legs had been splayed to an angle that must surely be painful, exposing their shaved quims, their fannies glistening pink.

Gagged and blindfolded as they were they could only guess at what was going on around them, but their imagination must have been working overtime.

As I watched them, the men surrounding the kneeling woman we'd just passed began exerting themselves upon her body. I heard her raised cries, which soon enough became gasps and then, later half-choked sobs.

At the sound of her, so near, the girls who had been tied on their backs, arched their bodies in fright and blindly craned their necks this way and that as if seeking the source of sound. Their clean, young limbs strained against the bonds that secured them. The movement allowed the lips of their virgin pussies to open even wider and I found myself staring at the deep, pink, folds thus exposed.

My arousal was becoming greater by the moment.

"They're kept blindfolded and gagged to heighten their excitement," the man beside me informed me. "Not knowing what to expect, their reactions to the first incursion are truly virginal." His voice was clipped tightly with arousal, and I had to just nod, not trusting my own tightly constricted throat to make much of a reply.

"Those three" - he indicated the other three girls that had been placed upon their stomachs - "they've been schooled a little bit. Virgins still, but they've had the tight little buds of their ass stretched a little. If you're that way inclined you can have sport with them a lot longer before deflowering them."

I thought of Soames' young serving girl, the way she'd been prepared by Malakai, and wondered if she was now one of these three girls, waiting for someone to come and use her virginal flesh.

"Shall we?" my new friend enquired. "Unless someone makes a start most of these men shy away from them. Virgins are sport only when you're alone. Their reactions tend to be totally unschooled and thus unpredictable. Most men here prefer to exert themselves against women they can trust."

He indicated with an outstretched hand and my gaze followed the pointed finger.

The group of men we'd passed on our way here had now

gone to work.

One was lying down on his back. The naked wench was sitting on him, her tight haunches placed directly over his erect penis. The man's hips were moving up and down and his member, what little we could see of it from this angle, was being driven in and out her ass.

What was remarkable in this set up was that as the woman was being pumped, her haunches invaded by the prick of the man she was sitting on, she had her legs splayed apart. Another of the group had arranged himself so that his penis was buried in her vagina. This man was holding her head by the hair, twisting it to one side, where yet another man stood, his hips pumping back and forth.

The woman's face was buried in this other man's waist, held fast in position by the man who was fucking her pussy. A fourth man stood on one side of her. He was holding her breasts and as I watched I saw his penis rubbing back and forth across her nipples, his hands crushing her bountiful breasts and the long arc of this man's milky juices flew to coat the woman's neck and breasts.

"Can you imagine any of these girls doing any of that?" my companion asked indicating the tied young virgins, and silently I had to concede that he had a point.

"They have to be gagged in case any man decided to mouth-fuck them first. I've never witnessed it but it's been said that for a virgin the first incursion of such manner, the taste of a man's juices, can induce a shock that causes their jaws to shut."

I shuddered quietly, and though I couldn't see his mouth I fancied my companion smiled. "So, shall we make a start?"

We advanced quietly upon the prone girls, who, listening to what was occurring around them squirmed all the more, unwittingly heightening the appeal of their helpless bodies. I watched my companion as he approached a tied girl who had been turned onto her stomach.

The girl's skin was the colour of burnt honey and there was an amazing smoothness to the slimness of her back, the fullness of her buttocks, rising like a couple of hillocks and the curve of her spread-eagled thighs.

My companion undid the thick leather belt that held up his trousers and doubling it he held it together in one hand, stretching it and testing its weight with the other.

He turned and winked at me. "To feel this again, the very first experience of pain and pleasure," he said.

As his outstretched hand caressed the girl's calf and ran all the way up her leg and the inside of her tender young thigh, she made a muffled squealing noise and squirmed violently against her bonds. The movement raised her hips off the bed. Her outstretched legs made the lips of her freshly shaved cunt separate, the fresh pink folds inside, glistened with the juices of youth and fear, and as she struggled ineffectually, the winking bud of her anus opened and closed at us.

Enjoying the girl's reaction, my companion moved his hand now so that he clutched at her unprotected cunt, his index finger slipping naturally into it, just deep enough to get anointed, but too shallowly to affect her virginity.

The girl squirmed even harder at this fresh assault. Her limbs thrashed wildly, restricted as they were in their movement and more muffled cries came from her gagged mouth.

"The thing with these girls," my companion explained as he withdrew his finger from her cunt and moving his hand over the fleshy, raised mounds of the girl's ass plunged it deep into the orifice of her ass and wriggled it about, "is that they think having sex is going to hurt."

There was more muffled squealing and thrashing from the girl and her reactions were making the others tied next to her react in a similar manner. He withdrew his finger from the girl's ass and stood up above her, his erection evident through the cotton of his trousers.

"Now, to prepare her to experience both," he said to me, and raising the thick leather belt he brought it down at full tilt across the girl's exposed buttocks with a satisfying fleshy sound.

The pain of it momentarily paralysed the girl, and as she began to recover and thrash about afresh my companion took full swing and brought the belt crashing down across her buttocks again.

The pain of it galvanised the girl. She tried to raise her head but blindfolded and gagged as she was, spread-eagled upon the bed she could do little enough that way. Unperturbed, my companion took aim again and swung down using his full body weight.

Each swing made a more satisfying sound than before, the honey-coloured skin slowly acquiring a darker tone. In truth it prepared, I thought, the girl for the assault that was to follow. The depth of the next pleasure that would furrow her little cunny as surely as this man's wide leather belt now furrowed her round behind.

My companion went on for some time. Swinging the wide leather belt onto the young girl's round ass, until it looked tender and sore.

It occurred to me that when in such state, every time she was fucked from behind, the merest pressure of a man's hipbones pumping against her ass would cause an exquisite sensation of pain for the girl.

What was it that Soames had said? Pleasure and pain. The two were somehow inseparable, one was always ready to turn into the other. That was the man's philosophy, and everything I saw here testified to its effectiveness.

"And now for the real thing!" My companion, tired at last of the sport with the belt, finally dropped his cotton trousers to reveal the monstrous girth of his erection and flung himself upon the defenceless girl.

The girl's moans and screams took on a new kind of pitch as the man gripped her pained buttocks in each hand, pulled the cheeks firmly apart and without hesitation thrust himself in full, up the tight button of her ass.

He pulled himself out almost immediately, spat in one open palm and rubbed it up and down his cock, winking at me all the while. "A little lubrication," he said, as he plunged himself into the girl's anus, his hips flattening themselves against the full round buttocks, causing her pain to mix with the pleasure of his taking her.

He worked himself furiously, his hips as they pistoned into the girl's buttocks, made a satisfying smacking sound of flesh on flesh each time he entered her deeply.

"Such a good fuck, such a good fuck," he gasped in rhythm, each time.

I watched as he worked himself into the girl, deeper and deeper, stretching the tight bud of her ass, and just when I thought he would finish, he withdrew his reddened member, its tip thicker and even more swollen with lust than even before he started, and grabbing the girl by her slim waist he raised her a little off the bed.

"Give me a hand here, see if you can roll her pillow under her hips," he said.

Fresh still from the incursion into her ass and the thrashing with the leather belt she'd received, the girl had gone momentarily limp in the man's arms.

I looked to where the man was pointing and seeing a pillow, I took it, folded it upon itself to make it thicker and then worked it under the girl's hips, between her hot flesh and the bed. Placed thus, the pillow raised the girl's private parts even more. The angle her legs had been pulled to and the rough use her body had just undergone conspired to relax the lips of her female orifice so that I could see the pink folds inside, the winking beads of moisture at her very centre.

"Do you want a go?" my companion suddenly asked and I was too stunned to immediately reply.

"Well?"

I pointed to the row of other waiting girls. "Plenty to go round," I mumbled and my companion shrugged.

He turned his attention to the prone girl once more, positioned the pillow under her carefully, and, mounting her from behind, he plunged himself into her cunt in one thundering stroke.

The girl's limp body came to sudden life. She raised her head as high as she could and arched her back and her limbs strained against their bonds so that every clean-cut muscle stood out cleanly defined under the burnt-honey skin.

Oblivious to this, my companion launched himself again and again, grunting each time, thundering into the girl's cunt with such force that each thrust drove her body deep into the bed's mattress.

"Have a go!" he yelled at me as I watched mesmerised. "Go on, Frank, have a go!"

The girl let out muffled gasps through her gag and her body shook violently.

Confused, I turned away from my companion, made my way away from the row of beds, just as a group of men heading towards them passed me.

Within minutes I could hear the slapping sound of leather on ripe female flesh and the choked gasps of pain coming through the girls' gags. The men were jeering, and as I looked back I saw them jovially bickering for position trying to decide in which order to have them.

I was still moving forward as I looked to see what the men were doing to the virginal young girls. My mind was confused as to what I should do, uncertain as to what I should feel, caught still between the twin grips of my sense of outrage and lust, and I stumbled upon yet another girl.

"Watch it!" I said, as I picked myself up.

"Master, I'm sorry," she begged and instantly prostrated herself before me. Unlike many of the women there this one I saw was dressed. Sort of. She wore a lace-up leather corset that held her body and hips but left her breasts exposed. Her bare legs were encased in knee-high boots of the same material and there were leather straps on her wrists and a wide leather collar around her neck.

She too had long black hair, tightly ringed, and her dark skin told me she was one of the lower caste. The sort of women I'd often seen sell themselves after-hours in street-corners in downtown areas of Rio.

She wouldn't look at me and as I looked down upon her I admired the slender cast of her shoulders and back and the widening curve of her hips as she abased herself in front of me.

The leather corset left her ass half exposed, and as I looked I could see the long lines of red already left there by some other man's belt or whip.

Perhaps it was the cries of the girls on the beds behind me being put to full use by the men, or the entire tone of the place, or even my own unfulfilled mood, engineered entirely by Soames, which finally took effect. The sight of this woman, ripe for the taking, abasing herself at my feet, made me forget entirely any misgivings I may have had.

"Up!" I said, and I was amazed to hear the thickness of my own voice.

I put a hand at the back of her head and, taking hold of her thick mane of hair, I half-raised her so she was on her knees in front of me, her eyes and mouth looking up at me.

"Master," she said obediently, and I marvelled once more at the training of all these women that enabled them to so calmly accept their fate and service any man, many men, as required.

"Here!" I changed my grip from her hair to the short lead attached to her collar and walked her on her hands and knees, like a dog, to a quieter alcove in a more secluded corner of the great chamber.

Decided as I was upon finally venting my lust, I was still determined not to do it in too public a manner.

The woman crawled on her hands and knees behind me, struggling to keep up with me, her full round breasts bouncing with the movement. When we reached the alcove I stopped and took better stock of her.

She was pretty, in the way that only the lower caste mulatto women can be. Her thighs, exposed from knee to hip, looked firm and nicely rounded, and as I studied her better I saw that the crotch of the leather outfit she wore was open, the lips of her cunt inviting intrusion. I put a hand out and cupped one of her breasts. It was firm and warm in my grip, soft and tender as I squeezed it, kneaded it, the dark rings of her nipples hardening in response as I caught their tips between thumb and forefinger and pinched them experimentally.

The woman took all this on her knees still, eyes downcast, breath quickening as I worked her flesh, so that her breasts rose and fell with each breath.

"Undo my trousers," I commanded, and beautifully trained as she was, she hastened to obey.

My erection sprung free.

"Suck me!" I said.

She took my thick member in one hand, slid it up and down the shaft, caressing it, and then her head dipped forward and her tongue snaked teasingly round the head of my penis. She coated it with saliva. The darting motions of her pointed pink tongue activated nerves just beneath the surface of the skin and sent shooting strains of pleasure coursing through my entire body.

So good was the sensation, so intense, that I fancied I would shoot my entire load in her face there and then, but she was too well trained for that.

The instant the slit of my pisshole was open and the first bead of salty fluid was out, her tongue quickly lapped it up. Her lips formed themselves into a perfect oval. They encircled the head of my penis and sucked upon it, increasing the engorged sensation I was already feeling there, while her long slender fingers formed a tight ring round the base of my cock and squeezed.

As the first spasms started to rock through me, the woman's right hand encircled the base of my penis and squeezed, stopping all fluid from getting through.

She waited like that, until the spasms had subsided.

I had my head back, eyes towards the ceiling, looking high overhead, seeing shooting sparks.

As the intense sensation subsided and I could look down again I saw the woman's dark ringed hair cascade round my loins as she drove her head forward.

The tip of my cock slid all the way into her willing mouth and her trained throat opened to take it in all the way.

From the angle I was seeing her, the double mounds of her wide ass beckoned enticingly, aroused me even further, and I dropped my hand down to her throat again, found the lead attached to the leather collar she wore, and tugged at it hard, to force her head against my middle.

She gulped, and I felt the stirring of her hot breath against the tight dark curls at the base of my cock, the hot trickle of saliva as she gulped me deep down her throat.

"Suck me deeper," I commanded, knowing it to be almost next to impossible.

The woman at my feet complied.

Gulping and gasping, breathing round the thick length of my shaft, she pressed her face hard against me. I felt her pretty chin brush my balls. The engorged testicles contracted at the touch and I instinctively pulled her head down harder to take the first splash of semen deep in her throat.

Dutifully, without needing to be told, she swallowed.

So long had I gone without release that the thick splashes overwhelmed even her capacity to cope with it and driblets of semen came running out the side of her mouth to wet her lips and coat her chin, and still I kept sawing my cock in and out of her mouth. I savoured the feel of it, splashing more and more of my load against the wet walls of her mouth with each stroke until I was completely spent.

I pulled back without letting go of the lead. Her face was flushed, her lips glistened wetly, and there were white droplets of semen on her chin.

I pulled her to her feet and turned her round so that her face was pressed against the wall behind her. Holding her thus I availed myself of her tender thighs, felt her flesh all the way up to the point where the inner curve of her thighs parted to reveal her snatch, and I massaged the well-used flesh there. She was hot and lubricated, doubtlessly by a good many other men.

I moved my hand a little higher.

Her ass, full and round, exposed as it was by the leather corset she wore, aroused me once more as I worked her flesh with my hand. I cupped the full cheeks of her ass and kneaded them. Squeezed them. Dug my fingers deep into the plump folds of her flesh. Then I looked down and slapped her ass once, twice, making the round cheeks bounce.

"I should butt-fuck you until you're senseless," I said, completely beside myself with lust. The very thought of the positions this woman must have been subjected to all night was threatening to send me over the edge.

"You are my Master," she said.

Crazed, I grabbed her snatch. Handled it fully until the centre of my palm revelled in the feel of it. I squeezed experimentally and she gasped. As I applied pressure with my hand she rose on her feet, came up on tip-toes, face pressed still against the wall.

I slapped the inside of her thighs, revelling in the soft feel of the flesh there. I parted her legs, exposed her cunt once more. This time I drove my index finger up her, as deeply as I could.

"Master!" she gasped.

"Shut up bitch!" I said. "Bend over!"

She put her hands flat against the wall, pushed herself away, and bent over for me. At the same time she arched the small of her back so that she presented me the best angle possible for a quick rear entry. The female width of her hips framed the centre of her open cunt.

I took hold of her hips in both hands and pulled her roughly towards me as I plunged the length of my cock into her hot went cunt.

The pink folds opened easily to take me in.

I heard her cry out in ecstasy but I had no time to think.

Cruelly I drove the full length of my swollen member into the centre of her body. Felt the double curve of her heart-shaped ass, form the perfect cushion for my pumping hips, as I fucked her from behind. All thoughts of morality and freedom of choice were momentarily eradicated from my mind.

I used her thus for what seemed like ages, but was probably no more than fifteen minutes, then her outstretched arms gave way. Her knees buckled beneath her. She cried out as her face was once more pressed against the cold hard wall, and as I came I reached out and cupped the full roundness of her free breasts, squeezed and crushed their tender flesh in my hands. I kneaded them roughly, feeling like a king, a stud, a conqueror of female flesh. I knew then the attraction of these orgies. I envied the Romans who must have had nearly a thousand years of it.

And with this thought my rod once more shot all its load in a willing orifice of this unknown girl.

5

My appetite for sex momentarily satisfied, I let my newly found sex toy fall upon her knees. She slid to the floor, with her back against the wall.

I realised then that my excess of passion had exhausted her. Weak from use, she was now fair game for any other masked man in the hall to find and toy with as he may please.

I made my way past women being taken by men in groups of three and four. The thought that I might partake in the sport provided, savour the feel of a well-used woman, did cross my mind, but for now, I decided against it.

So changed was I by my encounter with the anonymous woman I'd just used that I could now divert my attention to examining this grand chamber of exquisite pleasure more carefully. Despite the hidden mechanisms and state-of-the-art artifices that seemed to be everywhere in Soames' villa, lighting, I gathered was generally provided through smokeless torches.

Great trouble was in fact taken to ensure that the modern world intruded as little as possible upon the carnal pleasures of the men who came here.

It was as if Soames, having left his homeland behind, had sought to recreate a past in which he could hide. Not for the last time I wondered again at what heinous deed the Englishman might have been fleeing from.

Large as this chamber was, its walls were adorned with thick carpets of great plushness. It was this arrangement, I immediately understood, that provided a sound-dampening effect so that the voices of the many women being used didn't carry too far beyond the immediacy of their particular circle.

Obviously Soames had given a great deal of thought and supervision to the design. Despite myself I secretly felt a kernel of admiration for the Englishman. It was no easy feat to create a set-up such as this and keep it hidden from the eyes of the authorities for so long.

Some of the uses the women were being put to I had either seen myself or else heard being talked about. But inventiveness was obviously greatly valued by the patrons of this place, for they went to great lengths to devise novel forms of pleasure and unusual ways for taking women.

Indeed, my steps took me past a spot which illustrated that very practice. There, two men were engaged in the novel use of a totally black and tremendously well-endowed woman. The men themselves looked quite athletic. They had oiled their bodies, which were naked apart from the masks they both wore, to better draw attention to the flat stringy musculature of their torsos.

They reminded me of dancers, and I wondered if indeed this was not to be the case. There were a great many male troupes in Rio, and dancers too, I thought, were as prone to passion as any other ordinary man.

But it was the woman they were with that mostly drew my attention.

She had the blackest skin of any woman I'd ever seen, and the largest breasts - they were round and full, almost the size of water melons. The raised flesh round the nipples was almost purple and there was a lot of it.

The two men had stripped the woman naked. Her flimsy

clothing, such as it had been, lay in tatters around the two masked men, who were laughing lewdly to each other as they went about using her.

One of them, obviously the stronger of the two, was holding her upside down by the hips. Her pillowy breasts were pressed flat against his lower body, just below his flat stomach, and as he moved her this way and that, the erect nipples of her breasts rubbed against this man's torso.

His companion, standing on the other side of the woman, so that the twin full moons of ass were presented to him, was holding her legs wide apart, the flats of her feet pointing at the ceiling high overhead.

Thus held, the lips of the woman's shaven pussy were totally exposed to both men. The position in which her legs were being held looked uncomfortable, and she might have cried out except that her mouth was full with the erect cock of the man who was holding her by the hips.

As he held her like that, his fingers hooked into her flesh, he also moved her up and down, no doubt to increase the friction of her erect nipples against his lower body, and at the same time pumped his hips. The thickness of his erect cock slid in and out of her mouth.

In the meantime his companion was busy pushing a two-pronged dildo in and out of the woman's cunt. The dildo's second head entered the tight opening of her ass every time the man thrust it to the hilt into her vagina. She was making a low muffled noise, barely audible over the laughter of the two men.

From the way they were using the woman I gathered they were well-practised in the sport, and the woman herself appeared to be enjoying it. A prelude, doubtlessly, to what was yet to come, if I judged correctly by the array of other love-implements that were carefully positioned on cushions on the floor around the two men.

I looked back over my shoulder, squinting to make out the row of beds were the virgin girls had been tied up. I guessed that their virginity now was a thing of the past as each must have been taken by at least four men, and even as I looked I could make out a fresh line f masked men forming, trying to decide whether it would be worth their while to make further use of the tied girls.

Whatever reticence towards the various acts of passion these former innocents might have had at the beginning of the evening, I guess by now was long gone.

Through the poor lighting and the occasional writhing body that obscured my view, I saw that at least two of the girls had had their gags removed. One masked man stood at the side of the bed of one of them, bending his body forward no doubt to place the greatest part of his shaft inside the girl's warm mouth, and of the men I could see waiting more than one had lined up at the head of the bed for the same purpose. So, their training, I supposed, was showing results already.

The women around, it seemed, were used to being had by more than one man at any one time. Wherever I looked I could witness young beauties in varying states of undress, engaged in multiple couplings, their charms the exclusive property of the masked throng I now fully belonged to. I was joined to it by thought and deed, my loins as much on fire as any other man's there, all thought of high morals gone from my head.

In another corner I saw a woman, fully clothed, lying on her back and being enjoyed by two men. One of the men was kneeling by the woman's head, his knees on either side of her face. He was holding her legs by the ankles and was pulling them up high. The heavy material of her skirt had fallen back to expose long shapely coffee-coloured legs. Under the skirt she wore nothing, and like most women there her private parts had been carefully depilated, rendering the opening of her nether lips that much more desirable.

It was clear from the position she was being held in that she'd already been enjoyed by many a man tonight. The lips of her pussy had the swollen look that comes as a result of too much loving, a sure sign that her juices had been stirred by more than one cock already - and doubtless more were yet to come.

As I watched, one of the men positioned himself between the woman's spread legs, took out his own swollen member in one meaty hand, and with one swift thrust of his hips rammed himself to the hilt into her open-lipped sex.

As her warmth instantly enveloped him he started to thrust himself in and out of her. Each thrust was so hard that the woman's body moved along the floor every time he rammed her. The man who was kneeling by her head, and was holding her legs up so his friend could fuck her, also had his cock out - he could have easily pushed the bulbous head of it into the woman's eager mouth, but he'd chosen to do something different.

The woman's dress was low-cut at the front, her cleavage generous. It was into the soft sweet valley between her pliant breasts that this man now thrust himself. As his companion flung himself against her defenceless pussy, burying himself in her to the hilt each time, this man thrust his cock into her deep cleavage. Going deep each time, between the generous folds of the large breasts so that with each mighty thrust from him they bulged out even more and strained against the material of her tight dress.

I couldn't see the woman's face, but I could clearly hear the sounds she was making as the two men enjoyed her body, and I was left to no doubt as to her enjoyment of it.

Caught in this daze, fully satisfied with myself, sated at last, I walked like a wraith amongst the writhing bodies, each too deeply caught within the boundaries of its own private needs to be aware of my presence.

My mask made me invisible. Just another man amongst so many others. I could see that Soames' operation had a lot more dimensions than I supposed, and part of me marvelled at its full extent.

The polished, exotic girls that served as usherettes and fanned the flames of passion of the buyers upstairs had nothing in common with the common prostitutes I had witnessed in Soames' first display, the windows into other rooms he'd first chosen to show me, nor had the girls down here anything in common with the girls anywhere else.

And somewhere, in all this, I thought lazily, featured the girl of my dreams: Melissa.

It was funny that, now that I had sated myself on the charms of another, I couldn't get Melissa's special scent and body out of my thoughts. The thought of her being used by countless men, like the girls in here, made my blood boil, and a perverse sort of passion like a low-grade fever took hold of me.

It also made me more determined than ever to discover exactly what kind of hold Soames had on the exotic girl, for there only lay my hope of severing it and my chance to free her from him.

That there might be a selfish element in all these thoughts, that I might indeed wish to keep Melissa for myself, I did not permit myself to consider.

It was enough that here, on the first of my three nights as Soames' guest, I had experienced more and learnt more about his operation than would have normally been possible. I was not yet sure to what use this knowledge would be put but I knew well enough that all knowledge was useful and to possess it now rather than later gave me an advantage over Soames.

It was in the midst of these thoughts, when I was feeling cocky about my own power and beginning to consider the possibilities my action against Soames would take, that the realisation hit me.

The man who had so unerringly guided me towards the virgin girls had known my name!

The realisation pulled the rug of confidence from under my feet. Could it have been Soames himself? If so, then the entire's night work, all the experiences I had amassed, had been engineered by him and he was manipulating me. In order to gain - what?

The familiar confusion once more took hold of me. I felt deflated, my ego in tatters.

And it was in that state that I smelled her scent, that special mix of jasmine and juniper which could mean the presence of one person only.

I turned to see a veiled girl, dressed in the sheerest of silks, look at me with her golden eyes from not more than three feet away.

My heart beat faster at the sight of her and my lips were about to frame her name, when she brought slender fingers to where her lips would be in the universal signal for silence.

Her presence there further confused me, but it also gave me hope, hope that perhaps I'd been wrong and this night had not entirely been engineered by Soames. That there was more than one person's agenda afoot and that I still stood a good chance to make the devil pay.

Mesmerised, unaware even that I was moving, I closed the gap between us. Her strong scent was all enveloping. "Frank," she whispered.

I put a hand out and caressed her cheek through the thin veil, then, eyes drifting down to her perfect body, I felt in turn the double curve of her high full breasts, ran my hand down the side of her body, felt the slender waist, the seductive curve of her hips, round to the back to cup and weigh the double fullness of her buttocks.

She was perfection, unlike any I'd experienced with any of the girls so far. My hand, eager, questing, with a mind all its own, slid to the backs of her thighs.

"Not here," she said quietly so only I could hear, and I withdrew my hand guiltily.

Her very presence, the very feel of her flesh beneath my hand, had served to arouse me once more.

Around us men and women cavorted and writhed, and somewhere in this crowd, perhaps, Soames himself was exercising on the flesh of his sex slaves.

It all meant nothing to me now that I had found Melissa.

"Where?" I asked.

I had turned my back to her but for a second, to cast an enquiring look around, and when I turned back she was gone.

I looked madly around, eyes scanning, and saw the bare muscular back of a masked giant.

He was struggling with a girl, dragging her away and laughing. It was only the barest glimpse of golden silk that told me exactly what had happened.

Shouldering my way past groups of men busy having their chosen women, I chased after the giant.

"Wait! You! Wait!" I shouted, but my words were absorbed in the general hubbub. The giant continued to move away from me, shedding bits of golden silk as he uncovered his prize piece by piece, probably unable to believe his luck at such a find.

I continued to race after him, determined to stop him from using Melissa.

Upon realising the exquisiteness of what he held in his mighty arms, the brute must have decided not to share her with anyone, for even as I watched I saw him find a quiet alcove, not unlike the one where I'd already enjoyed the favours of my anonymous woman earlier, and dive in there.

Still quite a distance from him, I saw him push Melissa upon her knees in front of him. With one sweeping movement of his heavy arm he finished ripping off the golden silk that covered her.

With her body revealed, Melissa's beauty momentarily stunned him. He stood towering above her, unable to believe his good fortune. Then he quickly started to fumble with his trousers, intent to make her feel his cock inside her as quickly as possible.

Unable to match his strength, unwilling to draw attention upon herself, attention that could easily translate itself into abuse by more men, Melissa sat there quietly, eyes downcast, making no attempt to cover herself.

As I approached I too was enthralled by the perfect symmetrical fullness of her breasts, the long clean lines of her legs, the thighs filling out just enough to mark her as a woman, the slender waist and wide cradle of her hips, the unmistakeable seductive allure of her, the golden brown of her skin and the long hair cascading down her shoulders. It beggared belief that I had held that naked body in my arms, that I had made those lips part wide in order to suck me.

I promised myself that I was going to do so again. But first I had to get her away from this fool.

"Hey you!" I yelled, and the giant, half undressed, turned my way. There was thick, slabs of muscle on his upper body. A hairy chest and arms that wouldn't have looked completely out of place on a gorilla.

"Let her go, she's mine," I said.

He was half out of his trousers, his penis exposed and in no mood for talk. "Fuck off!" he spat out. He grabbed Melissa by the hair, dragged her towards himself and unceremoniously pushed her face towards his cock.

Speechless, I watched as Melissa opened her mouth. Her

tongue darted quickly, flicked along the length of the giant's thick shaft, touched it, tasted it, no doubt feeling revulsion but hiding it well, and then as the brute pushed harder, forced her face into his middle, her mouth opened wide, lips perfectly parted and, as she'd done for me earlier, she took him in all the way.

A wave of desperation washed over me. Physically, I was no match for this giant, so I had to find another way.

Melissa continued to pull with her lips and suck at the man's cock.

Masked as he was, he let out a gasp, and swung his massive hand downwards slapping her hard at the back of her head, driving her head forcefully even further forward so that she gagged, almost choked.

"Deeper! deeper!" he chanted, forcing her head down harder, grinding her pretty face into the coarse explosion of dark curls round the base of his cock.

I looked around.

Nearby stood a heavy bronze candle holder on a marble base.

I took it up and lifted it up in both hands. The thing was warm still, from the heat the candle had generated, and heavy. I staggered behind the giant, my makeshift weapon raised, and as his head arched towards the ceiling overhead with the excitement he was experiencing, I brought it down upon his exposed brow with all the force I could master.

He made a heavy strangled sound, a half-cry, and went rigid. His eyes bulged in their sockets behind the mask, as if they were going to take flight and seek new homes, and then he fell.

He fell like a stone.

Melissa was quick to divine what was happening and disengage herself. She pulled back from the man's body as he fell, and drew herself to one side, spitting in disgust at the forced taste of his manhood.

Despite the extremity of our situation, the enormity of the act that I had just perpetrated which could indeed serve to jeopardise the safety of both of us, I felt my eyes drawn inexorably towards the perfection of her charms.

Melissa crossed her arms in front of her attempting in a vain show of false modesty to shield herself from my gaze. But my mind was already busily engaged in devising new ways for her to appease me.

I crossed the distance dividing us in two steps. She had already put her veil back in place.

"Come," I ordered her brusquely, "let us get out of here. To a place where we may be alone."

Then, casting false modesty aside she took my hand, and leading me thus by the arm, masked and impervious, my eyes glued to the twin dance performed by the two halves of her tight ass as she walked in front of me, we marched to another alcove where was hid another doorway.

It was an exit out of this small part of Soames' domain and a tunnel that for me was to lead to new pleasures and a danger I never thought I'd ever have to face.

We entered the tunnel together. Inside it was completely dark.

I had, by now, become quite accustomed to the narrow lightless spaces that honeycombed Soames' complex, and so was used to the general lack of light within. Even so, thinking back, in every tunnel there was always a glimmer of light. Either that of burning torches in the distance, or else light seeping in from elsewhere, two-way looking glasses, perhaps, just like the ones Soames had first introduced me to.

I was determined now, in my thoughts, to get to the bottom of how and why my editor, as noble a man as they come, had come to be embroiled with a man like Soames.

In the meantime I was revelling in just being alone with Melissa. If only I could see her! This tunnel we had entered was the darkest yet.

The moment the well-oiled door behind us slid into place on silent runners Melissa and I were locked in otherwordly darkness.

The thing with darkness is that not only does it rob the eyes of their function, it also serves to heighten the senses. It was a device of pleasure as much of pain and that's why those young virgin girls had been tied up so securely, gagged and blindfolded, to increase their sense of helplessness, every young faculty they possessed suddenly ready to receive the rivers of lust all those masked men had been ready to pour upon their nubile bodies.

And now, I was not much unlike those young virgins, myself, in the dark, alone with a naked, masked Melissa. Every sense I possessed suddenly came to life in a way that I had not experienced for a very long time.

I became aware of Melissa's special scent. The ethereal smell of jasmine and musk that always marked her presence for me. The hard earth floor of the tunnel beneath my feet acquired new dimensions.

The crunch of the occasional gravelstone and the underlying smell of disused air told me that here was a tunnel that was not often used and had perhaps fallen into some degree of disrepair.

This thought put me in mind of the possibility of danger.

"Where are we?" I asked, as quietly as I could, uncertain just how far sound carried in tunnels like this. As it turned out my precaution was justified because the instant I uttered the words, the walls picked up the sound and amplified it, booming it along to the very end.

Instantly Melissa's hot, slender fingers were pressed against my lips.

"Quiet! Do not speak in here," she whispered against my ear.

Her scented breath sent little hot whirls of air to brush my earlobes and almost despite myself I felt a delicious shiver run down my spine. With my eyes totally blind, my extended senses were all too aware of the heat of Melissa's naked body pressed so closely against mine.

I could feel the hot touch of the outside of her thigh against my leg, as she leaned to press the fingers of one hand against my lips. Through the thin, cotton shirt I wore, I could feel the hard tip of a full, round breast inadvertently brush against my own chest.

These sensations, the heat emanating from her body, the feel of a tendril of her long hair brushing against the back of my hand, they all combined. I brought to mind the image of her perfect body and though we were in a situation whose outcome I could not predict, I was also human. To resist Melissa's charms, I'd decided long ago, would take a man who was more than human.

That man, I clearly wasn't.

I casually wrapped an arm round her slender waist and pulled her against me.

"Not here, not here," she whispered urgently, unable to raise her voice.

The special pleading, the urgency I heard in her voice, only served to heighten my arousal.

It was my turn to press my fingers against her lips, in order to silence her.

"Here! Now!" I whispered back into her ear, and felt the willowy body in my arms go still with resignation. It could be argued that I should have listened to her. Perhaps I would have done, had she argued a bit more strongly, so for what happened next she was to blame every bit as I.

The instant I had uttered my words she'd gone still. My

left hand, the one that was wrapped round her waist, dropped then, went down the ridge of her spine, revelling in the smooth feel of her soft skin, until it dropped to its destined target. Groping, it found and held one of the cheeks of her magnificent ass.

The very feel of it, its weight and shape, the hot smooth mound of flesh, submissive and pliable in my hand, drove me crazy with desire.

I had crazy visions of turning her over, grabbing her hips in my hands and spreading her legs apart in the dark, caressing her vulnerably exposed labia, before I butt-fucked that wonderful ass. But I knew that in the darkness, and the cramped confines of the tunnel, the experience would be neither as unrestricted nor as enjoyable as it would be in my own room.

So I dropped my roving hand further south, found the tight crack of her cunt, and roughly inserted an eager finger into the moistest treasure on Earth.

I felt Melissa's body stiffen. She didn't cry out, but her lips, where the fingers of my other hand were still pressed against them, opened immediately - and I felt hot, moist lips encircle their tips, a playful tongue dart against them.

Like before, I lost control.

My mind was immersed in a searing white heat that could not be blamed on my consumption of alcohol this time. I wrapped both arms round Melissa's body and pulled her roughly against me. I bent my head and buried it in the perfection of her proud breasts.

I teased and sucked and licked at them. My tongue tasted the very smoothness of her heated flesh and then ran a furrow from the depths of the scented valley between her breasts to the hard little tip that crowned each mound.

My hands, locked round her back, slid down the length of her slim body, until her buttocks were safely cupped in a cradle fashioned by my interlaced fingers.

Roughly, I lifted her towards me.

In the dark I felt the raised lips of her sacred mound press against the burning hardness within my trousers.

"Not here, please," she repeated urgently, but I was beyond hearing. I wanted nothing more than to impale this exquisite armful of woman-flesh upon my dick.

Beyond all reason, I wanted to debase her. Fill every one of her orifices with my semen. Hear her make that half-choking muffled sound as she sucked me deep down her throat. I wanted to feel the wet folds of her cunt close round my organ like a glove.

And then I would stretch the taut little opening of her perfect ass, force myself into her in a manner not unlike the way Malakai had rammed the handle of the riding crop into her. I would make her lick my balls until I was ready to come into her face and then I would have her take me deep into her mouth and swallow my entire load of come.

The intoxicating feel of Melissa's smooth skin, the resilient flesh pressed against me, the sheer perfection of every part of her body I cared to touch, consumed my senses with lust.

All I cared about, all I was focused on, was making Melissa mine - mine in every way.

I felt her slender fingers tug at my own clothing. I felt her snake a playful hand past the band of my trousers, intent on finding the source of all my most secret desires for her...

And then there was a blinding light.

And pain.

I heard Melissa cry out.

My fading hearing registered her cries of pain. The unmistakeable sound of female flesh being severely smacked.

My legs folded beneath me and a blinding pain filled all my field of vision.

I had time to register a smokeless torch being held high by a figure in blue: Soames.

Melissa cried out again and in vain I tried to focus.

My eyesight was all blurry, my head rang and the pain that had robbed me of all movement was growing, spreading with a force that was simply overpowering.

I let my head sink to the ground and darkness enveloped me.

And just before I faded, I heard Melissa cry out my name twice, before something was put into her mouth and she was reduced to making helpless, muffled sounds.

A thick-set booted foot descended by my head.

I had no strength to raise my eyes but I was in no doubt as to its owner.

Malakai had finally found me, along with Soames.

My last coherent thought was that my first night as Soames guest had truly now come to an end, and my own end would not be far behind it.

6

When I opened my eyes again I instantly realised that my fate had certainly taken a turn for the worse. I was in a kind of bare cell, stripped to the waist, and with my wrists and ankles chained in shackles.

There was a splitting pain inside my head, which in time I figured was caused by the blow Malakai must have delivered, but after a while I had gathered enough of my strength to focus around me.

The cell was roughly square, and of a construction as rudimentary as anything I could have imagined. There was no window and only a narrow door with a barred square opening. What feeble light there was came from a smokeless torch placed outside the door. The floor itself was untiled, of compacted hard earth, and dirty. The rough-hewn walls were also filthy with encrusted dirt of every description. Indeed, I had a difficult time reconciling it with the rest of Soames' villa, where everything had been kept immaculate by an invisible army of servants.

There was a hole in the wall!

At the furthest corner from me, artfully hidden within the shadows and the filth-encrusted colour of the wall, a roughly circular opening led to - somewhere else.

Normally there would have been no question about it. I would have stayed put. It's true, in the past my journalistic career had taken me into one tight spot after another, and my reputation had thus been made. But I had also learnt a vital lesson: trouble doesn't take long to find one. Therefore it is stupid to go looking for it.

But trouble, it could well be argued, had found me already. Besides, I was worried about Melissa. Her cries of anguish as I fainted rang in my ears and the thought that Soames was capable of almost any act, was enough to make me decide.

So, casting caution to the proverbial wind, I crawled on my hands and knees, painfully aware that my fine black trousers and once brilliant white shirt were now soiled with sweat and dirt, and stained by stains I could not identify. The hard-packed earth was painful to my knees, and my head was still not quite right after the blow it had received, but I crawled to the opening in the wall and tried peering in.

I might as well have been trying to look through the wall itself. A Stygian darkness lay within, and from it came neither light, nor sound.

I forced myself to venture into the narrow hole. The rough-hewn tunnel, for that is the best way to describe the opening

I found myself in, was big enough for me to crawl in as long as I remained hunched over on my hands and knees. Proceeding with as much caution as my restricted circumstances permitted, careful not to make too much noise through the dragging of my shackles, I crawled for what must surely have been a good hundred yards plus.

In the darkness it was easy to lose both a sense of direction and a sense of time. I neither knew how far I'd travelled hunched over like that, nor particularly did I care. Soon my knees felt as if they had little fires embedded in them, and, hunched over as I was, I could feel my shoulders beginning to cramp.

It was no surprise then that I didn't notice the grilled opening until I was almost upon it.

Clearly, the hole I'd just crawled through gave access to parts of Soames' complex he would rather have remained hidden.

Particularly from me!

Transfixed, with breath held baited, I peered through the narrow grill opening, which I now realised must serve as a ventilator of some kind, at the impossible scene beyond.

Everywhere I looked I saw women, shackled in chains much resembling my own, all being herded in long lines. There were white women here as well as brown, a clear indication, if any were needed, that this was part of Soames' enterprises that trowelled through Rio's poorest and most suspect areas, picking up in its dragnet as many down-and-out white women as coloured.

The women were dressed in ordinary clothes of every description. Cotton shifts and shorter dresses, almost threadbare, and they were all barefoot.

They were being herded into line by a group of Soames' ubiquitous coloured servants. As I watched I saw the foreman of the group, crack a whip this way and that, making the women cringe and cower, as they were separated into groups by looks, physical attributes and general comeliness.

One particular group of girls happened to be directly below the little grilled opening through which I was watching. They were all very young, probably none of them over nineteen, and all white.

A foreman in black trousers, his naked upper torso glistening with oil, moved this way and that amongst them, using the butt of his whip to either single out a girl from a group, or else move one in from elsewhere. As they were singled into line, the young girls huddled together, completely bewildered and as yet ignorant of the fate that was to befall them.

The foreman was a lascivious brute. His hands would tug at a loose piece of clothing as he went by, to reveal perhaps a young thigh, or else he would slap the suggestive outline of a girl's ass. Each time he did so, the unfortunate recipient would let out a squeal and gather herself into as tight a huddle as her shackles permitted, and those around her would also squeal in sympathy and try to mill around protectively.

The dark-skinned men watching all this would then laugh aloud and jeer and the foreman would have ample reason to further move in amongst the girls, separating them again and getting them into a line, his hands all the time taking liberties and eliciting fresh squeals and fresh cries of delight from his helpers and those watching him avidly.

Little by little, as this scenario was repeated, nubile bodies became more and more visible. As the hems of their tattered dresses became shorter and shorter by degrees, the long clean lines of their legs and thighs became visible and further fuelled the building lust of the men who herded them.

Through rents in their cheap clothing already one could see, part of the curve of perfectly shaped young breasts, the whole yet to be uncovered.

Basking in the admiration of his peers, the foreman pushed between two girls clasped in each other's arms. By their long blonde locks and smooth, frightened faces they appeared to be sisters. He put his whip aside and, seizing one girl roughly by her locks, he pulled her away from her sister, who let a high cry escape her at the action.

The foreman was deaf to the first girl's pleas as he pulled his prize along until she stood alone in a circle of hungrily-staring men.

"We've a beaut here," the foreman said, and the men clapped their hands with glee and pulled closer, crowding the cringing girl as he pulled out his whip and cracked it about, driving those nearest to the girl back. "No yet, no yet," he shouted as he did so.

The moment there was some space between the circle of dark men and the innocent-looking blonde girl, the foreman put his whip away again and turned to point out with his hand the young girl's comely attributes.

"Breasts like untasted pears," he shouted over the general level of noise. His hand went to the front of the girl's plain dress, grabbed a handful, and squeezed. The girl vainly tried to move back, but held as she was by her hair she could only shut her eyes and pray to whatever God she believed in.

Like a master showman the foreman waited, carefully gauging the mood of the men around him, and the instant it reached some kind of peak he reached out again with one massive paw and gripping a handful of the tight fabric straining over the young girl's breasts, he pulled savagely downwards.

The thin dress ripped in two and fell open in front in two halves. The girl let out a high pitched cry and crossed her arms across her front, gathering up the two halves of her dress to protect her modesty.

The effect she achieved was quite the opposite. As she

pulled the two tattered halves of her dress across her chest, where a pair of creamy coloured breasts threatened to spill out in plain view, the thin material whipped open around her legs and hips revealing underneath her complete lack of underwear.

I had heard of course of poor whites living in the lowest slums of Rio who were so poor as to not even be able to afford the most basic articles of clothing, and that this girl was one of them I did not doubt. She had smooth round-shaped thighs and the narrow hips of the young. The flat plain of her belly led down in a gentle curve to the magic place between her legs.

As she vainly tried to cover herself, the tattered fabric flapped this way and that revealing to the jeering onlookers that her sex had been depilated. The smooth plump folds of flesh between her legs lent an air of further delectability to the flesh now displayed.

Tiring of the girl's futile efforts to preserve her modesty, the foreman pulled harder on the tresses of hair he held in one fist. The girl's head was pulled back, and, unbalanced as she was, she milled her arms around to save herself from falling.

The two halves of the dress fell open, giving those around her a full view of high pert breasts, perfectly rounded, their peaks set high and tinged in pink. She cried out in protest and tried to cross one tender thigh across her front, but the foreman had expected that and taking hold of her knee he pulled her leg across so that for a moment she was splay-legged, the twin plump folds of her sex clearly visible.

Not satisfied with that, the man now turned the girl around and pulled the sad remnants of her dress down over her shoulders so that the smooth lines of her young back were revealed, and the twin full moons of her buttocks.

The buttocks shook as the girl tried to cover herself and

from the mounting jeers of the men I guessed what was coming.

"Mastah Soames say she for sale. She good for many men each day," cried the foreman and I looked a little more carefully at the young girl and saw the thickness of her ankles.

I remembered then Soames' discourse. According to his twisted beliefs this little thing was sufficient to tell who was going to do what, and I realised that the innocent young creature below me was destined for one of the water-front brothels. She would be worked hard, servicing dozens of rough sailors each day, and discarded the moment her beauty faded with the constant use she would surely be submitted to.

It was my guess that this side of business, the auctions held here, were less individually lucrative than Soames' lavish affairs upstairs, though probably not less profitable in the end, for clearly here numbers ruled rather than quality.

"What say you we try her a little? A taste before we're to bid?" someone said from the crowd of buyers, who must surely be brothel keepers from the more unsavoury parts of Rio.

A sly look crept in the foreman's face at this suggestion and he ran his tongue lewdly over his lips.

"Mastah Soames say no," he said, but he was already edging closer into the crowd of buyers as he said it.

A group of about eight of them had separated from the others and as the foreman ventured closer one of these men pressed a little purse full of coins in the palm of one massive hand. He made the bribe disappear by a sleight of hand and pulling out his whip again from the band that held up his trousers he motioned the shackled semi-naked girl to step forward.

She tried in vain to cringe back, but the instant the foreman stepped away from her the group of eight men fell upon her. She tried to turn and run away, but shackled as she was, she only had time to take one step before she was brought down to her knees.

She tried to vainly cry out as rough hands seized the soft tender flesh of the insides of her thighs and pulled her legs apart, revealing the pink depths of her open sex. Immediately one man shoved his erect penis inside her, his thrust driving his shaft in all the way and making her body rock with the force of the invasion of her.

Her buttocks shook as he started banging her, and her firm breasts jiggled with the backwards and forwards motion.

There were cheers of encouragement from those watching, and squeals of fear from the huddled groups of chained girls and women as they realised that they were all most likely to suffer a similar fate.

The girl would have cried out, but now her mouth was full with the thick cock of another of the men who had surrounded her. He was holding her by her blonde locks so that she couldn't move her head away and he was thrusting himself in and out of the pretty girl's mouth in a steady, metronomic motion.

At the same time another of the man had removed his wide leather belt and folded it to double length in one hand. He was watching the two men already busy using the girl and every time their thrusts coincided he brought his belt swinging down in a high overhead arc, so that it wrapped itself around the girl's bared back and exposed midriff.

The sound of the smacking blows of the leather belt landing heightened the half-muffled cries coming from the girl herself and made the men around her laugh harder.

No sooner had the two men using her finished their task and shot their load almost simultaneously into her than she was turned round, thrown on her back, and, with her legs forced wide apart, was subjected to another vicious assault between her tender thighs...

The foreman, realising he had a job to do, cast pleasure aside and turned his attention to the segregated rows of the rest of the girls. With all the buyers' attention now aroused, he cast his whip this way and that, landing it on female flesh with force sufficient to cut the thin fabric of the girls' clothes and make them squeal in pain, but not hard enough to break the skin and draw blood.

Soon all the girls and women present were in a state of semi-nudity, their comely charms in tantalising display, and the bidding was reaching a fever pitch, fuelled in part, no doubt, by the moans and cries of the blonde girl being used by the brothel owners.

But I had other matters to deal with - I left the sight of naked women and the sounds of their being subjected to the whims of their captors behind, and crawled towards whatever lay at the end of the narrow tunnel I was in. The darkness around me had barely had a chance to get as dark and dense as it had been before it again started to get lighter and I found myself heading for another tiny hole in a wall ahead of me without bothering to check it out very much, knowing that at this stage of the game I had very little to lose and my fate might indeed already have been sealed.

I knew too much! I had uncovered the vile means through which Soames ensured a supply of fresh women was always available and I knew how part of his operation worked. Low-level brothel keepers were given young girls and women from the slums, and at a different level girls were trained to become expensive sex-slaves, destined for a life of servitude to those wealthy individuals who could afford to buy the services of such exotic creatures.

Not satisfied with the money he was making in this fashion, Soames also had set up in his villa, his own specialised brothel. A place catering to a select few, one of whom I now knew to be my editor. And a special place in all this naked plunder was surely held by the organised orgies like the one I had taken part in.

Yes, it was beginning to come together for me now. The knowledge I held about Soames was beginning to give me a better picture of the man and his operation. At the same time I felt a degree of apathy inside me. A sense of inaction that was verging on the philosophical.

The pleasures I had experienced here, the special ministrations I had forced Melissa to give me, the depth of release I had achieved, all these had become like a key that had unlocked a different man in me. A man who couldn't care less about anything any more. A man who looked upon the possibility that his life might end soon, and all he could think about was the fact that he had at least experienced extreme emotions that would not otherwise had been possible.

It was a dangerous frame of mind to be in, one that could only lead to further trouble. But there was little I could do about it. Such was the fatalism that had suddenly overcome me, and with this last analysis of my own drives and motives, I crawled through the narrow opening I had come upon and tumbled into yet another dirty cell.

It was cell not unlike the one I'd just left behind, equally, cramped, dirty, of poor sanitary conditions and almost bereft of light except from the few sparse glints that found their way in via the rough-hewn barred opening in the door.

But small as this little cell was, it was already occupied by other inmates, unfortunates, no doubt who had, like myself, courted Soames' wrath. My companions, one man and two women, lay unmoving in a heap upon the floor in the middle of the cell.

Several moments of panic, silence and indecision followed my extraordinary discovery. Then I realised that they were asleep, lying in the middle of the floor, for the cell had no bed of any sort. The cell had no facilities of any kind for those most elementary bodily functions every man and woman must engage to on a daily basis, and which I would have rather remained private.

I spent a moment longer studying my prone companions, trying to ascertain whether they were going to be friendly or hostile

The two women were naked. They were both white. One was a blonde, with short, straight hair, the other a brunette, with long straight locks. At first appraisal they seemed comely enough, or they would have been had their bodies not been covered in smudges and marks of every description that spoke of a long time since they'd been able to cleanse themselves in any way.

The man who lay between them was dressed only in rags.

He was brown, a thin rangy kind of fellow of the sort I was used to seeing doing all the labouring by the port, carrying incredibly heavy loads all day under a blistering sun for a pittance. My appraisal of his social background did not last long, for as I sat there studying him his eyes popped open and focused upon me and I felt my heart begin to race.

The man's eyes were smoky, red, and sunken deep into their sockets, and as he lay sandwiched between the women, I noticed that, unlike me, his hands and feet were unfettered. A fact which put me at a distinct disadvantage should the fellow prove hostile.

He had one knee, firmly pressed against the blonde woman's crotch, the darkness of it contrasting vividly with the blonde pubic hairs she freely displayed there.

"Hi!" I said, testing them.

For long moments no one said anything.

At last the blonde woman lifted her head my way and in clear sounding English said: "What are you here for?"

A feeling of relief instantly swept through me at hearing English spoken like that. But how could I begin to explain?

How could I tell my fellow sufferers what surely they knew already? And yet, perhaps having experienced an altogether different side of Soames, the possibility remained that they may not the slightest idea what I'd been through.

As I thought all this the black man moved. He unwound himself from the two women's bodies and slapped the brunette playfully on the rump, as he got up.

"Move bitch," he said.

On all fours the brunette complied, getting out of his way with remarkable alacrity. Her breasts danced with the movement, their pointed peaks aimed at the dirt floor. The blonde also distanced herself from the black man, who standing now to his full height, revealed himself to be remarkably tall.

"Where are we?" I asked at last, deciding it was by far the safest question I could begin with.

"Soames' little playpen," the black man said. He was looking at me with a contempt I was sure I didn't merit, but I let it pass. My eyes busily took in the fact that of the two women the blonde one had the bigger breasts. It was hard to tell in the poor, light but her nipples were surely light pink as is traditional to those of her kind who have a fair skin and fair hair.

The brunette had the fuller ass. Wide hips and full, long thighs. Like the blonde, she had a full fuzz, dark coarse curls that exploded at the junction of her thighs and which she made no attempt whatsoever to hide. She stood with her back pressed against the wall, both hands held behind her, lifting her pert breasts even higher.

Incredible as it may seem, I breathed a sigh of relief. This was after all more of the world I had come here to find. A world different from but no better than the outside. A world which Soames ruled with an iron hand and a questionable morality and I had now come to reveal so that it may at last be openly questioned.

"What are you here for?" the black man asked again.

"I'm not sure," I said.

"Soames punished you?" he persisted.

"Not exactly."

"Then he wants to teach you a lesson." The black man sauntered towards me, and though I did not move my heart beat faster at the thought that he might indeed mean to assault me for reasons I could not even begin to imagine. I was about to bring up my shackles, use them as a weapon if I had to, when he abruptly stopped in front of me, legs splayed apart, then clicked his fingers, and the two women came off the wall and stood behind him.

"You're here for a lesson," he jeered. "Soames wants you to learn the meaning of power."

As he spoke the naked women behind him swayed and undulated. They ran their hands up and down the lengths of their torsos. Their splayed fingers moved over their rib cages to cup and caress their breasts in an obscene parody of love play. In my state, I found nothing erotic about their nakedness, their filth, the strange swaying of their movements.

To me they were just creatures. Creatures with breasts and cunts and open mouths, who apart from that bore little other resemblance to the exotic women I'd met until now. There was nothing in them of the strange seductive power that oozed out of every pore of Melissa.

Nothing.

"You want to see us fuck?" the black man towering above me asked.

No! I didn't!

I wanted to say no. I wanted, at last, to come out and say it. No! I did not want to go along with one more sick game devised by the degenerate Soames. I had no interest whatsoever in anything they might want to do.

In silence, my thoughts unstated, my mind choosing the

path of least resistance, I watched as the black man whipped off his clothes to reveal to me the full size of his arousal. He turned his back briefly to me, and I saw the long-faded welts left by the lash upon his skin. He had probably experienced the less than loving touch of Malakai's scourge before being left here to rot.

Oblivious to what he'd just revealed to me, he reached out with his left hand and grabbed the blonde woman by the hair. It was short, and he tugged hard, and she opened her mouth to cry out, but the cry she intended never reached her lips because the black man had been ready for it, and as her lips parted he slapped her with his other hand.

The sound the slap made as his open palm connected with her cheek was hard and dry, her cry dried with the shock of the blow. Then he brought his hand across her face again, going the other way, backhanding her.

"Watch this, white man," he said, and he slapped the blonde woman one more time - the blow was hard enough to bring her to her knees.

The light of resistance went out of her eyes then and she looked down at the filthy floor as the man pulled her roughly to her feet again, her full round breasts bouncing with the movement, their tips erect with pain.

He turned her round so that she faced the far wall. One sinewy arm wrapped itself round her slim waist and his other hand went to the back of her head as he pushed her forward, so that she was bending over from the waist down.

Even in the poor light I could see the involuntary parting of her thighs as he forced her into that position. I could see the framing of her cunt, its lips opening in response.

She did not struggle: her head went limp, all resistance gone.

The man looked at me now and gave me a slow wink as he ran his hand up and down the back of her legs, stopping just behind her knees, going all the way up her thighs, rummaging over the exposed moons of her bottom.

"This, white man," he rasped, "is the gate of heaven." His hand stopped momentarily over the crack of her ass, covering with the expanse of his palm the vulnerable opening of the blonde woman's anus, the vertical slit of her sex.

Then he raised his hand and slapped her ass.

The sound it made was identical in force with the slaps he'd given her on the face and her head briefly came up in pained response.

"Paradise," he murmured, and now he stood directly behind the blonde woman, supporting her waist with both his hands, his fingers hooked into her hips.

I realised he was about to use her. There and then, in plain sight of me, this revolting creature was about to fuck the woman he held in his hands.

The thought did cross my mind that I should do something. I should not once more become just another helpless part of whatever nefarious scheme Soames had put into motion here. But with the thought came awareness of my own true helplessness.

I was shackled. Half-dazed.

I watched helplessly as the black man suddenly thrust his hips forward. The tip of his penis parted the lips of the blonde woman's moist cunt with ease, and he buried himself deep inside her. His hips thrust so hard that the bony parts of his pelvis flattened themselves against the soft cushion of her round ass and a whimper escaped her lips.

Mesmerised, disgusted at my own secret arousal, I watched as he used her again and again, stopping at times to look at me. His hands ran this way and that over the woman's body, drawing attention to her ass, her thighs, reaching forward to find and cup her full breasts, slapping her if she moved as he squeezed her flesh.

And all the time he was buried to the hilt inside her. His hips sometimes slowed to an almost gentle, metronomic rhythm, at other times they blurred into a hard thrusting tempo that I was sure would split the woman in two.

And all the time, he spoke. "They all want to be fucked, white man," he said to me. "They want their pussy-lips parted by a cock. Their mouths filled. They live to please. Nothing more,"

As he spoke, he fucked. His rhythm was unbroken.

The brunette, all this time, had fallen back, thankful, I thought, not to be the one chosen for this session. But I was wrong. Her eyes, peering through the long black locks that fell in front of her face were fixed all the time on the black man, watching him closely.

Every time he stopped or even slowed down the brunette would crawl forward, the erect nipples of her breasts pointing towards the filthy floor, a pink tongue flicking over her lips. Each time the man resumed his thrusting she fell back, the light of disappointment evident in her eyes.

"Control white man," he said, "to fuck them is to control them!"

He had the blonde woman turned round now, on her knees in front of him, and I watched in sickened disbelief, for I knew what he planned.

As he spoke he seized her roughly by the back of her head and pulled her face forcefully towards his middle. I watched as she opened her mouth, lips parting wide to take him in as he forced her to pleasure him this way. He slapped her then, across her cheeks, two, three times, as she sucked him.

Perhaps it was too much. Perhaps the violent thrusting of him inside her mouth and the slaps got too much for her to bear. She tried then to pull back, but he was ready for this too. He pulled her head roughly forward, arched his back to thrust in deep.

"Suck it, bitch!"

And she obeyed. Arresting the backward motion of her head she leaned towards the black man, took his cock deep in her mouth. Deeper than I'd ever seen another woman take it.

It does my pride no good to admit that disgusting as I found this lewd debasing display, I also found the wet slapping sound made by the man as he thrust himself in the woman's mouth arousing, as were the slurping sounds made by her as she struggled to accommodate his length.

The perversity of it all had worked its trick upon the hidden beast that lies at the heart of us all, and my trousers ballooned with the evidence of my body's sudden betrayal. The man must have observed this, even as he used and abused the woman in his arms, for he clicked his fingers once.

Immediately, the brunette came away from the far wall where she had been waiting. She crawled slowly towards me on hands and knees, her eyes fixed hungrily upon my erection.

"And now for the finish," the man said. He picked up the blonde woman by the waist and lifted her off the floor and pushed her roughly against the wall, driving the air from her lungs as she flailed to escape his grip. Her arms moved helplessly over his back, her legs writhing in mid-air.

The black man timed it perfectly.

Turning his hips, he slipped between the blonde woman's writhing legs, pinned her to the wall.

His hips surged forward, buttocks pushing hard and judging by the fresh cry that was wrenched from the blonde woman's lips, I guessed that he'd found his mark.

Instantly, his pumping started afresh, each thundering stroke carelessly banging the woman's head and back against the rough cell wall behind her. But any compassion I could have felt towards her plight was now forgotten as I focused on the naked woman crawling towards me.

I let the brunette undo the front of my trousers and watched a pink pointed tongue caressed moist lips at the sight of my erect member. Then she brushed my manacled hands aside and dived in.

I'd been sucked by women before. Some had done it slowly, carefully. For some it had been distasteful. Melissa, had done it artfully, with practised ease, even as I'd forced her to take me deeper. The creature in front of me did it with an avidity that I found terrifying.

She took me deep into her mouth, deeper than I'd felt any woman take me, and moaning all the while she began to saw her head back and forth, her long, black hair swirling round my loins.

I felt the liquid fire being sucked up inside me.

Over the prostate body and bobbing head of the woman between my legs I saw that the black man had turned the blonde woman over now, so that she was on all fours. He was busy fucking her from behind.

My brunette's head rose and fell with incredible speed.

The entire tableau, the sight and sound of the black man and his blonde companion, the avid sucking sounds made by the brunette's oscillating head between my knees, all these mixed with the incredible physical sensations I could feel.

It all became too much and I exploded, splashing my load into the hot cavern of the brunette's mouth. I heard her slurping intensify as she struggled to swallow it all.

"Very good, very good! Excellent as a matter of fact!"

Soames' gloating voice brought me back from the precipice, exhausted.

Once more I was confused and disorientated.

Soames and the bulk of Malakai were standing at the open door of our cell, Soames resplendently dressed in white, the brooding Malakai, standing a step behind him, dressed in his habitual clothing of loose black cotton with a leather doublet. Soames was clapping his hands, beaming approval at us.

I felt shame at my weakness, and disgust for the way lust had betrayed me as I pushed the brunette away and gathered up my trousers.

"Thank you Mr Soames," said the man.

"Nice display, as usual," Soames said. Then he turned to me. "I'm sorry about the rough treatment, Frank. Melissa's kind of special to me. I sort of lost my temper back there."

I nodded, not knowing what else to do.

"We looked for you of course, back in your cell. Malakai here had forgotten about the hole in the wall. Our housekeeping down here, tends to be a bit poor sometimes." He motioned for Malakai, and the dark brute who so callously had beaten me senseless earlier, now knelt before me and released me from my shackles.

"What say you and me go upstairs, Frank?" Soames said. "Make a fresh start of your second day with us, hey? There's a new auction I'm planning today and your help will be invaluable to me." He helped me to my feet, threw a jovial arm around my shoulders, and led me away from the cell where I'd fully expected to spend the rest of my remaining days.

Though confused and disorientated, unable now to control the sexual beast that roamed loose within my breast, my feeling towards Soames had not changed.

I planned still to expose him.

Destroy all he stood for.

So my second day with him began. I had new insights into his strengths and weaknesses. I understood more about his methods. And I even knew a little of the men and women who came in contact with him.

"What auction?" I asked, playing the innocent.

He chose not to answer directly. "I think you will need a

bath and a fresh change of clothes," he said. "Not good for buyers to see you like this."

7

Getting clean was done the old-fashioned way. The ever present Malakai, his expression never softening towards me, supervised two men as they speechlessly brought in a large iron tub and placed it in the middle of my room.

"No hot running water then?" I attempted to make conversation with them, but they would not meet my eye. The instant the tub had been put down they retreated back down the dark passages they'd just come from.

"I take yar clothes," Malakai said.

There was no arguing with him. By his very demeanour I could tell that he didn't like me and would have loved me to argue. I took off my shoes and trousers, stepping out of them and leaving them on the floor for him to bend down and pick-up.

I remembered the scene at the dinner I'd had with Soames, and experienced a brief flashback of Malakai sodomising the servant girl, his thick penis being pushed roughly up her anal passage, his hands moving over her tender breasts, thick fingers squeezing and kneading the tender flesh. Her screams of helplessness had left me under no delusion that gentleness might be one of the components of this man's nature. To put this knowledge to a further test was not something I really desired to do.

The thought that, in the end, if I succeeded in challenging Soames and escape I might have to face Malakai's anger and physical power surfaced briefly in my mind, but I did not let it stay long.

I felt drained, exhausted both by my recent ordeal in Soames' playpen and by all that I had learnt about the man and his elaborate set-up. I could only really think forward to the luxuriant feel of hot water, which was soon to come.

Soames' argument to me of course did have an element of truth in it. I supposed that a great number of these unfortunates, did find with Soames a life far better than the gradual decline into drugs and cheap prostitution that would be their lot if they'd remained with their impoverished families. But to subject them to Malakai! Surely anything was better than that! And there was no disguising the fact that for every one of his girls who was sold to a wealthy man and found a life beyond her wildest beliefs, there were ten whose lot in this world were to fill the waterfront brothels, there to provide sport for the many men who came to use them, day and night.

My thoughts were interrupted by the sudden arrival of swarthy brown men. Like the ones who had brought my bathtub here they were thin, dressed in white, shoeless and silent. They each carried two buckets of steaming hot water which they now emptied into the metal tub. If my nakedness appeared at all unusual to them they gave no sign. Their eyes only briefly came my way, then, their buckets emptied, they turned and left.

"Not much for conversation," I said to Malakai, who all this time had been standing by the door with his arms folded across his broad chest. His menacing picture of guarded alertness was somewhat spoiled by my dirty clothes tucked under one massive arm.

"Thirty minutes," he said and departed. He didn't have a sense of humour either!

Alone now, I stepped gingerly into the bathtub. The water was scalding hot and as I had to ease myself in gently, by degrees, but eventually I was immersed in it up to my neck.

The hot water loosened the ache from my body, and

smoothed the bruises away. Its warmth had an almost magical effect. It freed my mind of all care, washed all worries from my brain and transported my imagination to a place I had never been before.

I imagined I was alone, in a room decked out all in velvet. Servants had laid out a table for me.

Seated in a magisterial throne of great comfort I watched without surprise as a door opened and in walked a veiled woman.

She was dressed in silks and satins that swirled and swam around her lush voluptuous body. Beneath the veil I could see that her hair was dark, and her almond shaped eyes almost hypnotic in their luminescence.

Without moving from my throne, I motioned with one hand, dismissing the servants.

The woman and I were left alone. From somewhere haunting violin music started playing and she waltzed to the middle of the room, now less than ten feet away from me. The movement made the swirling fabrics dance out around her and I could see she was barefoot. Where the silks and satins touched her body they tantalisingly moulded her full breasts and hard nipples, outlined the long lines of full curvy thighs.

She was exquisite.

To the sound of the music the woman started dancing for me. Her willowy body moved this way and that, her large unfettered breasts danced their own private message beneath her clothes. She arched her back and pushed her hips forward at me and through the thin fabrics that covered her I could make out the outline of a body made for loving.

Little by little the woman danced closer and closer.

I caught glimpses of bare flesh through rents in the silk, flesh the colour of burnt honey. She swirled for me, arms now held high as if she was praying to some invisible ceiling gods.

I reached out for her...

She was so close that my questing fingers touched the full curve of a buttock, before she swirled away again.

I wanted her.

Again she danced towards me. The captivating eyes above the veil firmly fixed on me. Her dance became faster and faster. The music picked in tempo, its rhythm increasing until the woman's body was a blur of motion, a complex puzzle of erotic glimpses of naked flesh and suggestive outlines.

I felt I was reaching the end of my patience. I wanted to stand up, seize this woman and fling myself upon her. Bury the burning need of my manhood deep in the soft centre of her fertile body.

So strong was my desire, so potent my wanting, that something of it must have manifested itself in my looks, for suddenly the woman stopped dancing.

The music faded.

"You can have me, Frank," she said, and the purring voice was that of Melissa. "You can have me, but first you must liberate me."

The cooling water around me helped me wake back into reality. I looked around my room. So vivid had been the dance of Melissa, the incredibly erotic quality of it, that I had to make sure that indeed she wasn't there in the room with me. The tip of my penis had broken the surface of the water and now stood to proud attention. I looked at it briefly, suddenly uncertain how much my present predicament was due to my passions and how much was owed to my professional interests.

It would be so easy to just do nothing. To let the next two days and nights pass without incident. No attempt to best Soames. No dangerous goading of Malakai. And when they were over I could go away and forget everything. Forget the available women, the sex-bazaars, the dirty cells with their perverse occupants. Forget all about Soames, Melissa...

Yet forgetting it all also meant leaving Melissa behind, and that was something I just could not do. If my recent dream meant anything, anything at all, it clearly meant that. I wanted to possess her perfectly shaped body. I wanted to be able to feel those incredibly hot lips wrap themselves around my own cock whenever I desired them. I wanted to pillow my head between her proud breasts every night. I wanted to feel her hips buck beneath me as I spread her and emptied myself inside her...

It was with this thought that I at last stood out of the bath, the water muddied and discoloured now with the dirt that had been on me. As I stood up, the door opened without warning and Malakai stepped back inside.

Surprised as I was by the brute's unexpected arrival, this time I kept my gaze fixed on his, challenging him to say something.

"Yar clothes Mastah," he said. He put a fresh pile of clean white clothes on the bed, along with a new pair of shoes. "Mastah Soames is waiting."

Despite his outwardly servile manner there was a note of challenge in his tone which I found offensive. He eyed up my still erect member with evident contempt.

"Mastah Soames say come now."

Malakai led me, like a dark shadow, through the beehive-like series of corridors that honeycombed Soames' elaborate construction, his broad back in front of me. I would have welcomed some talk, something to break the quiet padding of our footsteps, but he was not forthcoming and somehow I could not make myself press him on this matter.

I did wonder about the exact nature of his relationship with Soames, as well as on the perverse satisfaction he received from abusing all those young girls who came here.

Suddenly, without warning, he stopped and turned to me. "Mastah Soames have something special," he said, "he want surprise you tonight."

So astonished was I that I did not even have the chance to reply.

We had come to stand before a broad doorway. Twin wooden portals of an elaborately carved motif barred our way. He knocked once and then, turning sharply on his heels, he left.

Was that a warning he had given me just then?

Perhaps...

The great doors opened and Soames stood framed in the light that spilled from beyond the doorway.

"Frank!" he said, feigning surprise at seeing me there. He motioned his hand expansively, gesturing me to enter. "Come in, come in."

He was wearing all black. Black shirt, black trousers, black shoes. A black spider, I thought, inviting me into his parlour.

Sheepishly I entered, conscious of the vivid contrast my all white clothes and shoes created to Soames' black, and certain that once more this was no accident. The manipulative bastard did have something in store for me.

He ushered me forward into a chamber of truly immense proportions. If I'd thought the place where the last sex-slave auction had taken part was big, this room was truly enormous. Its walls were adorned with thick rugs that killed the sound. The rugs themselves portrayed intricate sex scenes direct out of the Karma Sutra. There were maidens being used by Persian Princes, in all different manner. Some women were turned almost completely on their heads, their legs pushed far apart to make it easier for the Princes to fuck them.

I realised then that I'd seen some of those positions enacted by the masked throng in the ballroom where I'd first found myself less than a day ago.

With the realisation I turned to Soames. "It was you, wasn't it? With the virgins tied to the beds, that night at the masked orgy?"

He would not admit it. "What are you talking about, Frank?" he said. He slapped me heartily on the back, drawing attention to the fact that the room we were in was packed. White men of every description lined the four walls, sitting in rows of three or even four, on either side of the door.

Music and incense once more filled the air, along with the expectant hush of lustful men about to bid top money for exquisite female flesh.

"What is it you really want of me?" I asked Soames.

The devil smiled once more and motioned for me to enter further.

"Circulate if you please, Frank," he said, "no way can I see to everyone of my guests alone."

And with that he left me.

I found myself alone in the crowd.

Once more troupes of the exotic looking brown girls and their Asian counterparts moved through the rows of seated men.

The girls were decked out in the customary short sleeveless tunics. Their bouncing breasts, bare arms and legs and the beauty of their faces served to heighten the arousal felt by every man in that huge room.

Some men were busy puffing away on thick Havana cigars. A corpulent gentleman to my right had stopped a girl and his right hand was going absent-mindedly up and down her smooth round ass under the short tunic, as he discussed something with the man seated next to him.

The muted sound of men's conversations, the sing-song quality of the girl's voices, the music, and the strange smells and sights and sounds were direct stimulants aimed at the weak spots of the beast within me, the animal which, by degrees, Soames' little tricks had uncovered in me.

I was righteous, in a way. More moral perhaps, if morality could ever be applied to sex. Perhaps even full of some strange zeal to do something for all these women caught in Soames' net, not so much out of the selfish need to project me as the crusading journalist as out of a possibly misplaced sense of social justice.

And yet, lurking within this complex array of instincts and creeds, there now resided a Frank Lewis who had taken part in a masked orgy.

And loved it!

Inside me was a Frank Lewis who wanted to take Melissa away from Soames because Melissa looked like a great fuck.

This Frank Lewis was as different from the man my boyhood friend Abu had so dutifully, if somewhat reluctantly, escorted in Soames' stronghold in the first place as, I guessed, Malakai was from any other man I knew.

The sight of so many easily available girls became far too much for that Frank Lewis to bear. Images of girls undressed, thoughts of what he wanted to do to them, passed through my mind in a flash, and before I could stop myself I had already acted on my instincts.

A girl passed me by, squeezing herself between me and two prospective buyers who had their backs to her. As she squeezed past, with that demure submissive look on her face and the feminine sway of her hips beneath the short tunic she wore, her thigh almost brushed against me. Reaching out, I seized her by one arm and made her turn back my way. "Master," she said immediately, her voice quiet, eyes downcast.

Her wrist in my hand felt delicate. Smooth and warm and fragile with the thin bones of a child, or an exotic. "You have a name?" I enquired coldly. Part of me was already reviling myself for what I was doing. But once started it was hard to stop and the very feel of smooth skin beneath my fingers was exercising its own intoxicating logic.

"Slave, Master," she was quick to say.

Slave indeed!

Holding her thus by the hand, I pushed past others, pulling her behind me, feeling her come meekly, the warmth of her wrist an intoxicating influence in my mind.

Not really wanting to be interrupted, yet knowing there was no private part in the hall and certainly no part Soames eyes and ears could not easily reach, I looked for a quiet corner, somewhere where I could explore the limitations of my control over both this girl and the beast that now looked out through my eyes.

I found a place by a large hanging tapestry against the furthest wall, and, leaning my back against it so that I could see what was going on around me, I pulled the girl roughly into the circle of my arms.

She did not resist me in any way.

My fingers dropped down her hair, revelling in its silky feel, then down the front of her tunic. She let me cup in turn and feel the fertile promise of her unfettered breasts through the thin fabric of the tunic she wore. I squeezed and rubbed her breasts through the material, teasing out her nipples, and when I had them I flicked each one with my thumb and watched as each nipple hardened in response.

Then I dropped my hand down her back, snaked it down the length of her slim doll-like body to feel the swelling of her buttocks.

Her ass was small, tight like a pre-pubescent girl's. I squeezed through the thin cotton, felt a firm buttock in my hand as the girl tensed to stop herself from crying out at my roughness.

"You like this?" I asked.

Her eyes downcast still, she nodded quickly.

Not satisfied with that, wanting to further test the power I enjoyed over her, I let my hand drop further, past the hem of her short garment. My fingers encountered bare flesh, the backs of her thighs, then slowly travelled up them, caressing the silky warmth of her skin...

I traced the smoothness of her with my index finger, down to that secret place where a young woman's thighs naturally part and the tight curve of her ass stops to give way to the female opening of her body. Her sex was completely hairless, as I'd expected it to be. The lips of her cunt were puckered, and as I touched them with the tip of my finger she almost jumped.

I ran my finger back and forth, tracing the vertical slit of her sex, feeling her tight naked ass pressed against my wrist and the twin pressure of her nipples through her tunic and my shirt as they were crushed against my chest.

"You have a nice cunt," I said to the girl, testing her.

"Thank you, Master." Her English was smooth. Cultured.

Roughly I pushed my longest finger inside her, felt the liquid smoothness of her cunt envelope it.

"I want to fuck you," I said.

At that the girl finally looked at me, her eyes truly terrified. I realised then the exact nature of Soames' plan on these shows. The freely displayed girls, the cigars and drinks, these were all designed to funnel desires, to feed the flames of lust that burnt in the buyers, but never ever assuage them.

Not before the auction!

I did wonder, of course, what would happen if a buyer did want to take things further. If one of them grabbed hold of one of the girls and did fuck her. I was sure now that such a move would not bode well for the girl. Men would be lining up to have a taste of her, Malakai's presence and Soames' other guards not withstanding. Besides, I was sure the ordeal the girl would undergo would be of much less concern to Soames than his customers' feelings.

"Is there somewhere we can go?" I asked.

"Master, you must not!" she said.

The warm pressure of her body against me, the wetness in which my finger was buried to the hilt, the whole charged atmosphere, these were having an effect upon me not much unlike the one I'd experienced initially when I came into Soames' villa for the very first time.

Perhaps, I thought, Soames was right. Perhaps he recognised the beast that lay deep inside me. The untamed monster that was now surfacing as my right hand closed around the girl's breast.

I couldn't fuck her, but I could use her. Her flesh was ripe. Warm. The thin fabric that covered her made her body all that more alluring to me. Its touch that much more forbidden and therefore more pleasurable.

I pulled back further against the wall and dropped both hands down to her hips.

Slowly I raised the hem of her short dress, bunching the material with my hands, up round her waist. Her stomach was flat and smooth, the flesh supple and young, with the soft dawn of a baby. The slope of her smooth belly gave way to the valley that led down between her legs, where the tops of her tender thighs curved out. Her sex had been depilated and the very look of it excited me almost beyond reason. She had plump hairless lips, soft folds sticking up like an adolescent's. I licked my lips in anticipation of what I could experience with the body of this girl.

So engrossed was I that I failed to notice the approach of a man behind her.

The loud slap of flesh on flesh, the tensing of the girl's body and the suppressed gasp as she bit her lips to prevent her crying out where the only signals of warning that I had.

"Not a bad piece of ass."

I looked up to see a man about my age. Tanned, dressed in white and wearing a Panama hat.

He grinned at the surprise he could see on my face.

"Sorry to startle you, but this girl's hot fanny just happened to catch my eye."

He smiled at me directly over the girl's head, and one more I felt her body stiffen. I realised then that this man had just inserted his finger into her vagina and was busy savouring its velvety feel, just as I had been moments earlier.

"This must be your first time," he said. "We're not allowed to fuck the girls on the floor. The good stuff will turn up later."

I let the girl go, pulled her away from the man's hand and pushed her on her way.

He watched the swing of her hips as she walked away with a wistful expression on his face. "Pity, she really was a good piece of ass. You got a name?" he asked.

"Frank, Frank Lewis," I replied feeling stupid.

Around us the atmosphere was fast reaching the critical point where the carefully stoked passions of the buyers would require release and only the auction of the girls they really came here to buy could assuage them.

"Jim," my interlocutor said.

"Just Jim?"

He grinned broadly again and looked around quickly. Despite the crowded room we were in, the area where we stood was relatively isolated. Jim took a long Havana cigar out of his shirt pocket, carefully chomped the end off and spat it on the floor, then lit it using a gold lighter.

"Abu sends you greetings, Frank," he said through the smoke of his cigar as he exhaled, and before I could reply he smoothly moved away.

I stood there, rooted to the spot, as Jim took a seat at a

prominent position amongst a circle of noisy buyers. None of those around him spoke to him, but then again he didn't try to speak to them either. He just sat there, fitting in.

Either he was a message from Soames, a reminder that unless I behaved myself Abu would come to instant grief, or else my boyhood friend had managed to find a way to help me out of my predicament.

And as if to punctuate the momentousness of this very last thought, a gong shouted a single deafening note and the whole room descended into stillness.

The auction, I realised, had begun...

This time Soames had outdone himself. The girls that were trooped out into a protective circle were dressed in snippets of leather that barely hid the nippled flesh of their breasts and preserved the modesty of their sex.

Each had a loop of thin gold wire round her waist and from this were suspended triangular pieces of leather that attempted to cover their front and back. I say attempted because as they moved the triangles moved with them, occasionally giving tantalising glimpses of the pleasures that would be stormed so many times tonight by so many.

At the back the triangles did little to hide the sexy curves of each girl's backside. The material just fell vertically into place, managing only to conceal the tiny button of each girl's anus and the junction of her thighs where her sex was.

If anything this attempt at modesty further accentuated the magnificent curves of their plump round asses, so that as each girl started to dance and gyrate to the sound of ethereal music that came invisibly from a hidden alcove somewhere, the hints of their charms became tantalising glimpses.

Amongst the girls moved Malakai.

The brute had stripped down to his trousers, displaying massive arms the thickness of tree trunks and a torso smooth and hairless, oiled to show off its impressive musculature.

In one hand he held a whip, and he cracked it skilfully as the girls fleeted around him, making them jump and squeal but never getting close enough to mark any of them.

The buyers seemed to like this display, for each time Malakai cracked his whip and the girls he aimed at squealed and jumped, their protective triangles at the front would leap also, and their breasts would jiggle and threaten to spill out of the triangular scraps of leather that were holding them constrained.

Then came a lull in the music.

Malakai straightened up and looked expectantly to the left and to the right as if he was searching for someone.

The buyers waited with bated breath, obviously having seen this before.

Sure enough, out of the far left corner, amongst clouds of swirling smoke from a fog machine, came Melissa.

She was dressed like the other girls, in scraps of leather. Her proud breasts, scooped into the tight halter top, threatened to spill out with every breath. Her long legs and thighs were already promising a taste of honeyed Paradise to every man who sat there watching her, mesmerised by the sinewy movement of her perfect body.

To me, her appearance acted like a stimulant. I felt the need to possess her once more, to do more to her than I had ever done to a woman. I remembered Soames' displeasure with her, and the thought did cross my mind, that this time he might decide to sell her indeed...

The thought made my heart begin to skip faster inside the cage of my chest.

To free Melissa, to possess her for myself, this had now become my prime motive. It would of course be just like Soames to divine this and pre-empt my plan by selling her off to someone else now.

Holding my emotions under rigid check, I moved along the line of buyers until I stood beside Soames, by the large blackboard where the girls' names had been written.

Next to Melissa's name he'd chalked in a large star, and next to that a number had already been written in.

The bidding, it appeared, had already began.

Soames caught my eye, and, as if reading my thoughts, he flashed me a wicked grin. "Hope you're enjoying the show, Frank?"

"Is there nothing here I can do to put a stop to this?" I asked needlessly. I already knew the answer to that.

"Frank, Frank," he chided me in the mock manner a schoolteacher reserves for a child. "Have you learnt nothing so far? Have I taught you nothing? You don't really want to stop all this."

"I do. I do!" I said it as forcefully as I could without raising my voice. I wanted to believe I did. I wanted to believe that I was different to Soames, that the beast that ruled me went by another colour to his.

"No, what you want is to do to these girls," he pointed with his chin at the troupe of girls waiting expectantly around Melissa, "what you did to that usherette earlier." He grinned again. "And worse!"

I tried not to show my embarrassment and irritation. Was there nowhere safe from this man? And if he was as omniscient as he appeared, then surely he already knew what I planned deep in my heart.

"Frank, watch this!" With a faint movement of his hand, he made the girls around Melissa fall back into a semi-circle. They knelt where they stood. Bowing their beautiful heads and folding their legs beneath them in the half-lotus position, so that the bountiful cradles of their hips fanned out. The scrap of leather dangling over their shaven sexes barely preserved their modesty.

It was done so masterfully, with such calculated grace and poise. Another of Soames' ways of increasing the already considerable allure of these women. And yet, the instant I looked at them, my rational judgement clouded over and I felt my vision blur with lust.

I knew then what went through the mind of each and every buyer in the room with me. To have one of these heavenly creatures as your property, there to perform whenever you wished, to do whatever you commanded of her. It was a thought that could drive any ordinary man to distraction.

"Every buyer in this room is already calculating how much to spend on them," Soames whispered by my ear. "Everyone! But that isn't enough. I want them ready to go over the top. Spend wildly for the pleasure of having the exclusive use of each of these delightful girls' hot bodies. Such pleasures shouldn't come cheap, should they now Frank?"

I shrugged, unable to take my eyes off Melissa.

She was the only one now standing. Alone. In the middle of the troupe of girls. She was looking somewhere over the heads of the buyers and though I was desperately willing her to make eye contact with me, she seemed to be lost in some private universe of her own.

"Gentlemen," Soames said in the ensuing silence, "let the bidding begin," and with that he motioned to three servants standing behind me.

I realised that many of the buyers would use these servants to ferry their bids back and forth, thus preserving their anonymity, and I marvelled again at the sheer complexity of Soames' set-up.

The instant the bidding began, the music started playing again and Melissa began to dance. Only this was like no other dance I'd ever seen from her. Lost as she was in her own private world, she locked her eyes to the ceiling overhead and stretched her slender form to its full height, intertwined her slender fingers and raised her arms straight above her head.

The pose drew attention to the pure dark marble pillar of her neck and it made her full breasts bunch together, almost overflowing the skimpy top.

From where I stood, watching, I could feel the tension in every breath of the people around me.

My feet and those of the other onlookers had taken us all to a vantage point. Crowded us together, all on our feet now, none wanting to miss the spectacle presented.

I wanted to glance over at Soames, see what he was doing, what he had prepared for me here. But I could not take my eyes off Melissa, so entranced was I by the sheer animal magnetism of her, the sexuality of what she was doing with her body.

Her fingers danced downwards, travelled the smooth length of one extended slim arm, to come and rest on the swell of her ripe breasts. From there they travelled back up her neck, over her chin and she slowly inserted each finger in turn deep in her mouth, her pouty lips sucking on it, her moist pointed tongue coming to lick her lips after each finger had gone.

All the time she was doing that she was throwing her hips forward. The muscles beneath the flat plain of her belly, would tense and spasm and the movement of her pelvis being thrown forward so suddenly would make the little triangular leather flap that protected her sex from our lustful eyes jump up.

There was a collective from the onlookers each time there was a brief glimpse of the vertical slit of her sex.

People around me, those who were either sharing my line of vision or else were on either side of me, tensed and fidgeted in their chairs. Those others who had been unfortunate enough to be standing or sitting elsewhere craned their necks and asked those around them if they'd really seen her cunt.

I could feel my heart pounding. Inside I was torn by the attraction I felt towards this strange mysterious girl.

As if sensing my own arousal, Melissa suddenly dropped her head, her eyes focused on the crowd.

Holding her body rigid she moved her feet on the spot, in time to the music, and as she made eye contact with me, the flats of her hands went to the inside of her thighs. Slowly she drew her hands up the curve of her inner thigh, towards the part of her covered by the leather triangle.

There, she let both hands disappear under it.

Men all around me were transfixed, their eyes almost bulging from their sockets.

Slowly, slowly, Melissa arched her back, her body bending backwards, towards the floor, her flowing black curly locks sweeping down behind her.

The movement made the triangle at her middle rise higher, and every man in the room could see Melissa's index finger, inserted deep in her vagina, moving in and out, wet and slick with her secretions.

The generous mounds of her breasts pointed towards the ceiling, their nippled tips clearly aroused and erect.

I swallowed to clear my throat.

I was entranced.

With the same sinewy slowness as before, Melissa straightened up her body. She withdrew the fingers from her vagina and brought them to her mouth where she began to lick them slowly, running the tip of her tongue from their very tips to their base and then up again.

It was a brazen display of sheer wantonness, even for this place, and I was amazed at the capability, the casual power over men's carnal desires that Melissa possessed.

Then she straightened up.

From behind the troupe of sitting girls, now appeared a

black man I initially mistook for Malakai. He had the same thickness of body and arm, only his face was scarred. Long lines of faded stitches ran from the very top of his shaved head to the tip of his chin.

The dark skinned man was dressed in tight leather trousers which drew attention to the outsized bulge of his manhood within. His chest was wide and hard and long slabs of muscle ran in ridges across his stomach.

He pushed his way past the sitting girls, his thick muscular thighs brushing them aside effortlessly as he pushed by. As the tempo of the music increased and a heavy drumbeat was incorporated into it as he came up behind the unaware Melissa.

So sudden was this man's appearance, so monstrous his manner, that even I, knowing it all to be a part of a carefully orchestrated act, found my chest tightening with expectation at what was to happen next.

Before the brute could quite reach her, as if sensing his very presence, Melissa turned.

Her hands flew to her face in horror and she made to flee, but the man was too quick for her. He reached out a massive arm and grabbed her hair in his thick hand. Melissa, let out a pained cry as he pulled her off balance and she fell towards him.

With effortless ease the ugly giant turned her at the very last minute so that she was crushed against his heavily muscled chest. Her willowy form was encased in his thick arms, her back pressed against him. Her exquisitely beautiful face now carried a look of genuine terror.

I saw her look pleadingly at Soames, and turned my gaze on him.

He saw me looking and winked at me.

He was smiling.

"It's just a show, isn't it?" I asked, suddenly feeling a deep sinking feeling begin to develop at the pit of my stomach.

"Relax Frank," he said. "Enjoy!"

Another cry wrenched from the beautiful lips of Melissa made me turn my head back to her. Holding her imprisoned within the circle of his arms, the brute with one powerful motion had ripped the skimpy top from her. In vain she attempted to cover the sweet round orbs of her breasts.

Slowly, grinning, the giant brushed her protesting hands aside and cupped and weighed each round mound. He squeezed and fondled the firm ripe flesh, bringing her nipples up. As his hand travelled from one breast to the other, there were buyers around me who chomped hard on their cigars while others dropped their hands on their laps, to surreptitiously massage the ache beginning in their groins.

Powerless against the giant's strength, Melissa allowed him to use her like that.

The man persisted at playing with her perfect breasts for a few moments longer, then, no longer satisfied with that, his hand dropped down to the triangle of leather covering her crotch and with another swift motion that raised another pained cry from her, he ripped that away too.

Melissa now stood naked, her perfect body revealed.

There were feverish eyes all around her. Male faces engrossed on what was about to take place. The man put his hand around her neck then, the fingers encircling it almost completely, and holding her thus he displayed her at arms length.

We were treated to the sight of a perfect behind. The two globes of Melissa's round ass, perfectly symmetrical, flared out to the sides, the deep cleft in between them inviting further use. Where her ass joined the tops of her full shapely thighs, the twin moons of her ass curved tightly and gave way, forming a diamond shaped opening that was the entrance to her sex.

The sight of her so helpless further inflamed the men around me and cries of encouragement were raised.

"Go on, give it to her!" someone yelled directly behind me and the cry was taken up by others round the room.

"Fuck her ass."

"Make her suck you."

"Mouthfuck the bitch."

"Show us her cunt."

Melissa cringed to hear them all bay like that.

I turned to throw another enquiring look Soames' way, but the Englishman was busy listening to one of his house boys giving him some rich man's bid.

Desperate, I turned back.

The giant had forced Melissa to her knees in front of him now. I watched helpless as he slapped her across the face a few times, each time her hair flying out with the force of the blow and her breasts jiggling with the motion. Then he extracted a massive penis from the front of his leather trousers and in plain view of everybody he placed the tip of it into Melissa's mouth. Too stunned from the heavy blows to resist, Melissa opened her mouth and took the swarthy man's cock in.

The crowd around me went wild.

"Deeper, deeper!"

So different was the atmosphere this time from the orderly affair of the first auction I had witnessed that I looked around in amazement. The usherettes had fallen back against the far wall, too afraid to venture now amongst the sex-crazed men. The prices chalked up by Soames on the blackboard were fast reaching astronomical heights, and the girls of the rest of the troupe were watching the display of Melissa with a blank ashen look on their faces that finally convinced me that this was no part of the show.

This was real!

I looked back to see Melissa had finished sucking the man off. He pulled his still erect member out of her mouth and took hold of her hair yet again and forced her down on all fours. On her hands and knees with thick droplets of semen upon her face and lips, Melissa turned to look for help.

If Soames saw her desperate plea, he chose completely to ignore it.

Goaded on by the crowd around him, the man took hold of Melissa's hips. His massive paws lifted her knees off the floor, and instinctively Melissa brought her legs together, trying to deny him entry into her body, but he forced his massive thigh between her legs from behind and pushed her knees apart.

Then he swivelled his hips, so that he positioned himself between her legs. Her body now helplessly imprisoned in his arms, he held her by the hips, her long shapely legs on either side of him, unable to bar entry into her cunt.

"Stick it to her!"

"Make her cry!"

The crowd chanted around me, and to my eternal horror and shame the sight of Melissa's beautiful body, her hair falling in waves over her face as she was held, her hips raised to give the man easy entry, was starting to arouse me also.

It was almost too late...

"Soames!" I shouldered my way past the heaving chests and pressing bodies of the men immediately around me. "Soames!" I cried again, making my way to where the Englishman stood, chalk ready in one hand.

Behind me I heard Melissa cry out in pain and the man give out a heavy grunt that left me in no doubt as to what was happening.

"Soames!"

"What is it, Frank? Aren't you enjoying the show?" He turned my way with an infuriating smile on his devilishly handsome face.

"Have you not got enough?" I pointed at the astronomical sums of money that had been chalked up next to all the girls' names. I didn't fail to notice that they had all been sold, this time. The only one still being bid for was Melissa and the sums put up for her already amounted to more than I could earn in four years.

Soames surveyed the figures on the board with a raised eyebrow.

Behind us Melissa cried out again and I heard the crowd roar its approval.

"Please," I said. "Please!"

"So I was right," he said. "The bitch has visited you!"

There was a venom in Soames' voice when he spat out the words that made me cringe and almost fall back. But another cry from Melissa and the heavy slap of flesh hitting flesh emboldened me to go on.

"Let it go," I said. "You've won."

"Won? Won did you say Frank?" Soames seemed genuinely amused by the notion. "Tell me then, what exactly have I won Frank?"

"I won't publish anything, not a word!" I said. "Nothing!"

He smiled then. The feral smile of a demon who knows he's won his bet. "But you wouldn't anyway, you fool. You know you wouldn't. What would you have said? That during your stay at my villa you fucked and used a girl in an orgy and felt the soft ass of a servant? Or would you write that I hold poor white girls in concrete cells and you discovered one while her cellmate sucked you off?"

The bastard confirmed my every suspicion there and then. Everything had been planned from the start.

"Why?" I asked.

"Why what?"

"Why all this?"

"Why corrupt the only investigative reporter left with enough balls to come into my den and unearth my operation? Is that what you're asking Frank?"

A fresh cry from Melissa, behind me, made me turn back. Through the closely packed backs of men, I had a brief glimpse of her naked body being lifted up in the air like a rag doll, legs splayed apart and powerful hands round her waist pulling her down to be impaled upon a monstrous penis.

"Please stop this," I said again in despair.

"What are you willing to offer then, Frank?"

"Offer?"

"The bidding is still on." Soames indicated the blackboard with the astronomical sums next to Melissa's name.

"Any longer and there'll be hardly anything left to bid for," I said.

"Nice try Frank. Melissa can take worse than that. Trust me."

He could have been bluffing. Maybe not. But Melissa's desperate cries sounded genuine enough for me not to want to call the Englishman's bluff.

"What do you want?" I finally said.

"Your soul!" His face loomed close to mine. "Your soul Frank. Nothing less will do for me now."

I pulled back in horror. He grinned at me, showing his small, even teeth.

"You devil!" I hissed and it only made his grin grow wider.

"You don't know the half of it, Frank."

I turned away from him. My view of Melissa was being prevented by a solid wall of men's backs. They were all straining forward now, getting as close as they possibly could. Quite a few of them had their hands buried deep in their pockets, their elbows moving up and down.

From where they were looking I could clearly hear the rhythmic slap of flesh on flesh and agonised groans coming from Melissa's mouth, and the cries of the men were an unmistakeable guide as to what exactly was going on:

"Stick it to her again!"

"Fuck her senseless from behind!"

"Make her ass cheeks wobble!"

Melissa was making half-choked sobs, the breath being driven forcefully from her lungs as each time she cried out.

Maddened I turned back to Soames.

"My soul?" I asked.

His grin never faded. "Nothing less Frank. Nothing less."

"All right then!" I said furiously. "You shall have it. And be damned!"

Without looking he reached out behind him and unerringly drew a white chalk like across Melissa's name on the board.

"You're the one's who's damned Frank," he said. "She's my creature, you know. She's always been my creature."

8

I ran from the auction chamber like a man possessed, not knowing exactly what selling my soul meant nor where I was heading and not truly caring either.

My only thoughts now were of Melissa.

Doorways and passages I could not remember opened to right and left. They led me down narrow corridors and to unfamiliar sights. It was as if Soames' villa could at last reveal to me its nefarious nature, show me its otherworldly character in a maze of newly-formed corridors and ever expanding space.

I was lost. Lost in more ways than one.

What would Abu make of me now? I thought of his well-meant advice which I'd chosen to disregard, and his reluctant help that got me into this mess in the first place. It brought to my memory the strange man back at the auction, the one who'd approached me as I fondled the firm flesh of the usherette's ass.

'Nice piece of ass.'

Jim. His name had been Jim.

Hell, Abu had many friends. Influential friends. Was it possible that he was making some attempt to get me away from Soames' monstrous clutches? That was a role Abu had played many times before we grew up and he became a wealthy trader and I a journalist. In the distant past, our boyhood adventures had been marked by my being caught in one scrape or another and Abu bailing me out at the last possible moment. This time, though, he would be too late. He would come only to find Frank Lewis damned forever, and for a woman!

That would amuse Abu, Abu who valued women for their services but always complained about their cost. Well, his boyhood pal had just about paid with his soul. The ultimate price! How's that for cost?

So deeply lost was I in my thoughts, so completely unaware of where my feet were taking me, that when I finally focused my thoughts enough to look around I found myself in a semi-circular area, an arena with doors heading off in five different directions.

There must have been a dozen doors...

I contemplated turning back, but as I was no longer sure which way was back, and as I really had come to feel that at last I had nothing more to lose, and thus little to fear, I decided to make a choice and keep going ahead.

I reached out and took hold of one of the door-knobs. It was circular, made of brass, and as I touched it it felt cold beneath my palm.

I twisted it and entered into another world.

Unlike the narrow smoky corridors I'd left behind, light here was provided by electric bulbs.

There was a short passage, nicely carpeted, and three more doors - left, right and ahead.

Doors, doors, doors. If anything had become the trademark of Soames' place it was doors. Doors and hidden passages that led behind walls. Secret mirrors and Melissa's cryptic warning that there were more doors in this place than met the eye. The bastard must have spent a fortune burrowing into the hillside behind his villa, turning it into a molehill inside which lived and breathed a thriving community. An empire of the senses, overseen by this vile beast.

Without thinking about it I pushed the door and entered another room and here I stopped short.

It was a spacious bedroom.

One of the plushest I'd seen.

A large king-size bed covered in silks dominated the room. There were rich carpets on the walls and the floor and a large fire-place in a corner provided a moody, romantic atmosphere unlike anything I'd experienced or come to expect even in this place.

Electric lights were everywhere. A chandelier overhead. And mirrors. Mirrors in the ceiling above the bed. Mirrors in the wardrobe doors and on one side of the bed.

I knew the room instantly for what it was: a love nest of some kind.

Absorbed in my observations, bent on cataloguing the cost and wealth of all I saw there, it took me a moment longer before I noticed the room's occupant.

She was a young girl, no more than twenty.

She was sitting in front of a large mirror brushing her long blonde hair and she had her back to me.

Careful not to make a noise, I closed the door behind me,

and with my thumb pushed up the latch that held the door in the locked position.

The girl was quite unaware of my presence. Her body was covered by a short silk robe held together by thin straps across her shoulders. Her skin shone with a smooth creamy quality, and as her right arm moved back and forth dragging the brush through her long silky hair her unfettered breasts rose and fell. Their pink tips pushed against the transparent material of the robe, clearly visible in the mirror from where I watched her.

She had on a satin pair of black panties that matched the colour of the robe and contrasted beautifully with the creaminess of her skin. Her breasts were softly rounded, their tips slightly erect, no doubt from their friction against the fine silk of the robe.

As I looked at her from behind, I could admire at once the flaring curve of her young hips and the tight roll of the taut flesh of her ass. The firm cheeks of her backside disappeared inside the black material of her satin panties.

Her legs were crossed in front of her, but from the side I could see the long smooth line of a young thigh, the shapely calf and dainty foot ending in painted silver toenails.

I cleared my throat.

"Is that you, Edward?" she asked, in a high childish voice, the inflexion and tone clearly English.

It was the last straw.

The idea that this heavenly creature was Soames' little secret, his special girl, brought all the way from his distant homeland, maddened me. It was clear that she was his property, like Melissa, but obviously better prized, kept away from other men, there to please only him. Exclusively. A tender reminder perhaps, of what he'd left behind.

I took a single step towards her.

She saw my reflection in the mirror then, and turned round

with a scream. Her hands dropped the pretty brush she'd been using on her hair and tried to hide the sweet fruits of her breasts from my gaze.

In vain!

I saw that the robe ended approximately at her hips. The flat smooth plain of her belly shone through the sheer fabric, and as she turned, her legs uncrossed, the thighs opened and I caught a brief arousing sight of the vertical cleft of her sex, the raised lips of her labia briefly outlined against the black satin of her tight panties.

"Who are you?"

She sounded outraged. No doubt she was used to ordering Soames' servants about and having her every whim obeyed at once.

I crossed the distance separating us in three strides and seized hold of one of her arms.

"Your worst nightmare!" I said. I was surprised at the strength of anger I could hear in my voice. "I'm your worst nightmare!"

Already, before I hauled her on her feet, the form my revenge against Soames would take had been decided in my mind. I'd seen the way he had reacted at the thought that Melissa, whom he regarded as his property, might have visited me in private. He just couldn't stand the idea that I might have fucked her. Sullied his property perhaps, or else used her without his express consent. Whatever strange code of honour he applied to justify the use he made of these women's bodies had obviously been offended.

It was clear that he prized property. He considered the women who belonged to him to be sacrosanct, used or not only at his whim, and I was about to prove to him this was not the case.

"Get up!" I pulled the girl on her feet and dragged her roughly towards the bed.

"Who are you? What are you doing?" She tried to resist, fear not yet evident in her voice. She seemed certain that this was all a big mistake and a word from her would be enough to stop me in my tracks.

"I am the man who'll fuck you senseless, you spoiled little bitch!" I hissed, and had the pleasure of seeing some real fear cross her eyes and mar the perfection of her features.

"Stop. Please stop!" The movement she made as she resisted me made her delectable breasts bounce enticingly through her silk robe and I felt the first painful rise of lust in my groin. "Please stop. Edward will kill you if he finds out."

"Let him find out then," I said. I pulled her off balance threw her onto the bed, where she fell in a tangle of limbs, face down. Her arms flailed as she tried to regain her balance and scramble on her hands and knees, but I was upon her instantly.

I seized her by the back of her head and forced her face down on the sheets. With my other hand I hooked my fingers into the sheer fabric of her silk robe and pulled roughly downwards. The thin material parted with a thin tearing sound and the young girl's body was revealed.

Her back was slim, and muscled with youth. The deep ridge on either side of her spine disappeared into the twin double haunches of her ass, inside the black satin of her panties.

"Please, please!" I could hear real pleading mix with the fear in her voice now but I was remorseless, high on anger and desperation and willing to do anything to wound Soames.

"Please, don't hurt me. Don't hurt me," she repeated. "I'll do anything, please don't hurt me."

So she had not been on the learning end of Soames' philosophy on pain and pleasure, the bit about the two being one, each enjoyed only when experienced in conjunction with the other.

Pity!

But she would learn!

"Anything?" I asked, and her reply was muffled because I was still applying pressure at the back of her head, pushing her face into the sheets of the bed.

"Anything, anything!" she repeated, and I laughed.

I brought my hand down and slapped her ass, pleased at the sexy way the tight cheeks of her saucy backside quivered with the force of the blow. Her flesh felt smooth and warm under my hands. I was beginning to enjoy the abuse I was about to inflict upon her.

"Let's begin with this then," I said tersely, and slapped her backside again, harder this time.

She tried to cry out. Tried to turn and fight me. But she was only a slip of a girl and I was much too strong for her. I had only to increase the pressure I maintained at the back of her head to reduce her cries and screams to muffled whimpers.

I paddled her hard, on her black satin covered ass, revelling in the firmness of her flesh, and the slippery feel of the material that covered it.

Then, when I judged she'd had enough, I stopped and pulled back. She went instantly limp on the bed. She probably thought that I'd had enough, that if she pretended she was unconscious I'd be satisfied.

She was wrong!

I was just beginning.

I ran my right hand, up the back of her shapely calf and felt the silky smoothness of her skin as she tensed.

My fingertips traced a path onto the back of her knee, lingered a moment on the sensitive skin there, and then moved purposely up the inside of her thigh. She realised where I was heading and tried to bring her legs together, but I'd been expecting it and was too quick for her.

I reached the junction of her legs just as she brought them together to protect herself, trapping my hand in the sweet prison of her thighs. My fingers pressed tightly against the raised mound of her sex. It felt slippery and warm through the satin, and I massaged it gently, rubbing her up and down, feeling the raised lips of her labia and the entrance to the sweet warmth of her body.

She whimpered and tried to wriggle from under my grip, but I just increased the pressure at the back of her neck, immobilising her from further resistance.

"Spread yourself," I ordered, increasing the pressure of my hand at the back of her neck.

Instantly she complied.

Her delightfully shaped, young legs fell apart.

She remained totally still, submissive to my exploring touch.

My fingers, given free rein, rubbed her crotch up and down a few times, and then, eager to taste more of what was on offer here, I pushed the thin satin material of the girl's panties aside and dived in.

I'd been right. Made to flow by pain and panic, her cunt was lubricated and warm. I pushed my index finger up her, revelling in the slipperiness of it, and then withdrew it to run it over the lips of her labia.

She shrunk away from my touch and tried to squirm on the bed. But her struggle only made her saucy backside wriggle more provocatively and the slim round thighs opened wider with her efforts.

The sight inflamed me further.

I withdrew my hand and seized the thin black satin of her panties and pulled at it hard until the elastic snapped and the material ripped away. She gave a muffled wail and one of her hands flailed behind her, trying to bar me from enjoying the sight of the sweet gate to her body.

Maddened with thoughts of revenge, and now lust also, I slapped the hand away.

Momentarily I let her go, released my tight grip upon the back of her neck and I pulled away from her and loosened my clothing. Before she could recover enough to make a move, I was upon her again, my body completely crushing hers. My weight drove her deep into the mattress of the bed.

Her ass where I'd paddled her was tinged a deep red and as I fell upon her the erect length of my shaft rubbed between her hot tight cheeks.

"Please, please," she was saying all the time but I couldn't care less about anything she said now. I just wanted to use her.

I came on my knees behind her, took hold of her legs by the ankles and roughly pulled them apart, splaying them wide, ready for me to penetrate her. The lips of her cunt opened up with the sudden movement, the pink wet folds inside opening like a bud about to flower.

She tried to pull away from me, using her hands, but I just yanked back on her legs and her entire body rushed to be impaled upon me.

The instant I entered her she screamed.

I felt my shaft slip all the way inside her with the first thrust and I dropped my entire weight on her unprotected body, uncaring whether I hurt her or not.

I used her like that for several minutes, enjoying the whimpering sounds that were being wrenched from her. Then I pulled away from her with a sudden wrenching movement that I was certain had hurt her.

I turned her over onto her back. Her young breasts pointed at the ceiling, her tight pink nipples were hard with shock and fear. My hands gripped her legs from behind the knees and I raised them high until each leg was on my shoulder.

Trapping her thus, immobilising her with her legs apart,

I surged forward, my entire body's weight on her, and as I thrust anew upon her cunt I could enjoy the expressions of pain and helplessness that fleeted across her pretty face.

With her legs trapped on my shoulders, I bore forward until her knees were pushed against her chest. My thrusting hips could feel the tight cheeks of her ass as I rammed into her. And such was the extent of my raw anger with Soames that with each thrust the body beneath me moved upon the bed and the cries of agonised passion that were being wrenched from her lips were a sweet sound to my ears.

My hands descended upon her upturned breasts and gently I cupped each soft mound. I squeezed them gently at first, thoroughly enjoying the feel and texture of her skin, the exquisiteness of her barely used flesh. I bent forward to taste her nipples, my tongue circled them madly, insistently. As I bent to enjoy my fill of her body's sweet peaks my entire body surged forward and my hips rammed even harder against her unprotected ass. My shaft slid deeper into her with the movement, and she cried afresh at this deeper invasion of her body.

"Cunt!" I shouted at her then, "we've only just began!" And I had the pleasure to see the look of resignation that took over her face at the prospect of a prolonged bout of pleasuring me. The very thought of what fresh use I had in mind for her, was enough to make her body go limp beneath me. I enjoyed her submission, and to mark my rights over her I thrust again as hard as I could, and though she stubbornly bit her lips to stop herself from crying out, a cry was still wrenched from her.

I held myself from coming yet. I had not finished with her. I pulled away from her body, revelling in the silky feel of the inner walls of her cunt. My shaft was mightily engorged, shining wetly with her juices.

I made her sit up.

Her breasts joggled freely with the movement and I slapped them to make them bounce harder. I repeated the blow from the other side, revelling in the pain I was inflicting on her.

She tried to cover her breasts with her arms, tried to cross them over in front of her chest, and I slapped her hard on the face, made her hair fly about just as that brute of a man had done to Melissa earlier in the evening.

The force of the blow made her roll away from me across the bed. But before she could recover and think of escape I had her by one ankle and I was dragging her back. I back-handed her across the face to stun her and then slapped her breasts again to make them bounce some more.

"Please," she tried to say, but her spirit was broken and it only came out as a whimper. I hooked my fingers in her hair, took a good grip of it, and, hauling her to her knees so hard that she cried out again in pain, I pushed her face down, towards the erect tip of my cock.

She had no time to avert her face. Her head went down towards me. Reaching across her bent body with my free hand I slapped her ass again and she opened her mouth to cry out, only this time it was filled by my cock and she gasped and almost choked on it.

I pushed her head down hard, feeling the tip of my cock brush hard against the back of her throat, and when I felt her try to pull back and gasp for breath, I pulled her back by the hair and slapped her again.

"That's for Melissa!" I shouted as the flat of my hand landed across the seductive little face. I picked her up, my hands still gripping her hair, and forced her to go down on her knees beside the bed.

Soames had taught me well I thought, as I used the ripped shreds of her robe to tie her hands high up behind her back. Then I then grabbed a sheet, ripped two long pieces off it and tied each end to a leg of the bed, then took hold of her ankles, and as she was kneeling I pulled them roughly apart and tied each one with a piece of the sheet.

Tied up like that, kneeling down, legs uncomfortably far apart, she was mine to do with as I wished.

I came up behind her and my hand clumped on the tight cheeks of her ass again. Her flesh was soft and smooth and firm, crying out for further use. And as she was helpless like that I took hold of each cheek and pulled them apart to expose the winking orifice of her ass.

She tried to wriggle in protest. "Please, no!" she had time to gasp, before I rammed my penis up her ass and her cries of pleading were reduced to moans of pain and protest.

I stretched her little rear passage for some time, feeling the tightness build up the passion in me, and then when I knew I was ready, I withdrew my swollen member and stood up.

Pushing her head down on the bed. immobilising her completely, I rammed my erect penis past her pretty pink lips, red and swollen from her biting them, and splashed my semen inside the hot walls of her mouth.

She struggled to swallow it all. Her eyes widened with the shock of it and she tried to cry out again, but all that she made was a gobbling, half-choking noise and then she went limp.

I pulled out slowly from her mouth and let my softening member, its tip glistening still from her combined saliva and my secretions, play upon her reddened lips and rub itself against her cheeks, leaving a wet trail behind.

She had fainted.

Tied up as she was, she looked most delectable. The sight of her vulnerable backside put me in mind to use her again. To thrust my cock up her ass again. To feel the tight lips of her cunt close around me as I shafted her from behind.

But the anger that had driven me was fading now. I

straightened up my clothes and left the girl tied up, well-used and senseless, as I let myself out of her bedroom and looked for a way to get to Melissa's room.

My use of Soames' little playmate had left me more drained than I'd thought. Its cathartic effect had not only taken the edge off my anger against the Englishman but also slowed my wits.

So I was totally unprepared for the sight that greeted me as I finished traversing yet one more of the interminable corridors and pushed open a heavy oak door.

Behind it was a group of women in different states of undress.

I realised instantly that it was a sort of communal room, for there were scattered tables and chairs and dishes with half-eaten food everywhere. A smaller table was laden with backgammon sets and dartboard-like targets had been set up on a couple of the walls. A knife or two stuck out of at least one of them.

All this I saw in a flash, but what caught and held my attention were the activities the occupants of the room were currently engaged in. The men were all natives, and judging by the few items of clothing some of them still had on their persons they belonged to the servants' caste that took care of everything around Soames' villa.

The women were totally naked, freely displaying their charms. Some of them were down on all fours. Others had been laid out on their backs, with their legs up in the air. One or two had been pushed face down against a table, or alternatively sat upon it so that their fannies were available as they leaned back and spread their legs.

The women were being subjected to every conceivable sexual position possible. And what's more they seemed to like it.

I saw one man sitting on a chair, his shirt open to the waist, his trousers down around his knees, while on his lap a naked brown woman jogged up and down on his shaft.

The man had his face buried in the woman's ample breasts and he was busy massaging them with his hands and lips. She had her arms around his head and was pulling his face tight against her chest.

She was moaning as she bounced up and down on the man.

Everywhere I looked there was more of the same.

The bonded members of Soames' working underclass were clearly enjoying themselves every bit as much as their master, only with a lot more pleasure and a lot less pain.

I was about to backtrack out of the room, go out the way I'd come in, when one of the women being taken from behind suddenly noticed me and let out a scream.

Such was the quality of her shrill cry that instantly every member in the room ceased whatever carnal activity he was engaged in and looked around to locate the source of her discomfort.

I felt their eyes settle upon me.

A couple of the men disengaged themselves from their women's bodies and without bothering to restore their modesty reached and out and pulled a knife each from one of the targets on the wall.

"Ya chose wrong door, Mastah," one of them said, so quietly that I almost didn't hear him.

Several of them advanced towards me with an unmistakeable gleam of hate burning in their eyes.

"Look, I can explain," I stuttered, but I could see that they were not interested in explanations.

Trapped here, in their dens, I was sure that the servants would waste no time in venting all their anger on me. And the very thought of what form this venting would take made my legs go rubbery and my knees tremble so that I was rooted to the spot, unable to take another step to protect myself as they advanced upon me...

"Stop!"

An unmistakeable voice had shouted from the shadows, and I thought how strange it was that I should feel relief at seeing Malakai again and hearing his heavy tone.

Sure enough the dome-headed brute advanced towards me. He parted the people in front of him like so many leaves blown in the wind.

He also was in a state of undress, evidence that he had been disturbed whilst he was taking his pleasure, and the thought of this served to weaken me even further - my situation, I reflected, was worsening by the second.

"None of that," boomed Malakai's voice and for once I felt gratitude towards the man.

The people around me fell back, melted to the corners of the room, as Malakai advanced towards me.

"Yar out yar depth here, Mastah," Malakai said and I looked to determine whether he was just toying with me. Whether he indeed, intended to do me more harm than any of these other poor souls could.

"I guess I fell out a little with your Master," I said.

Malakai advanced towards me until he stood directly in front of me, his massive chest and arms and shoulders attesting to the power of his body. Then, without a further word, he put a massive hand on my upper arm and silently led me out of the room.

I waited until we were back out in the corridor and he had closed the door behind him before he spoke again. "Mastah Soames not like ya," he said.

No prizes for guessing that, I thought to myself.

"Mastah Soames fear ya."

Melissa had said the very same thing, and it puzzled me.

What could I possibly do that would make Soames be afraid of me? It was all academic of course. Whatever it was that I could have done, the devil had now won. I had pledged my soul to him, and whatever that might mean in the long term it left me in no doubt that in the short term at least, I'd lost.

"You know the deal I have made with your Master?" I asked.

Malakai nodded slowly, his domed head bobbing up and down in the half-light. "Three days, three nights. Enough time ta loss a soul," he said cryptically.

"I think I already lost mine, and I've still got one more day and night to go," I said to him. "Not the kind of thing that would cause your Master to fear me, wouldn't you think?"

He seemed to consider my words carefully before replying. "He afraid. You not weak. Just slow to see."

"Slow to see what?"

"The power. The strength in vice."

Cryptic prattle, I thought. But perhaps he did have a point. Or at least I could use his belief to get away from here.

"Your Master -" I said. "If I win, if I manage to defeat him will you -" I meant of course to ask him if he would let me get away, but at the last possible instant the thought sprang into my mind from nowhere and I said instead: "Will you serve me?"

"If ya win," Malakai said, to my surprise and consternation. "Mastah Soames treat all people like dogs. He no sense of respect."

It was strange to hear mention of respect coming from the lips of the hulking giant who'd done nothing but terrify me since I entered Soames' household. The very same man I'd seen abuse Melissa at the beginning and sodomise a servant girl at his master's orders.

Still, it wouldn't do to question him too closely. If suddenly he was to be my ally, I could use every little bit of help

I could get.

"I need to get to Melissa," I said. "I'm lost."

For a reply Malakai reached out at a spot of the wall directly over my head and pressed his fingers against it. There was a click and a whirring and a section of the wall slid smoothly back to reveal another passage.

"Melissa down there," he said. "Mastah Soames with her." He pressed a smokeless torch into my hands.

"Your master's got a little blonde playmate stashed away up here," I said. The gleaming domed head bobbed up and down again. "I paid her a little visit. She's all trashed up and tied to the bed. Warmed up in every way."

I had the pleasure of seeing a great wide smile bloom on Malakai's normally sombre face before the wall panel slid back, hiding him from view.

9

I made my way through the narrow lightless passage to which Malakai had directed me. It smelled unopened, full of stale air which told me that the passage itself was not often used, and it was so dark that I was thankful for the smokeless torch the giant had given me.

My thoughts, as I walked, were equally divided between what I would find ahead and the use Soames' sex-mate was probably being put to right now by the servants. The brief glimpse I had of Malakai and his friends at play had given me the impression that they would be inventive at their sexual games, willing to subject Soames' special girl to everything at least once.

Such was the true nature of the sex beast unleashed inside me that despite the apparent hopelessness of my situation, the thought of the blonde girl servicing all those men fired up my imagination, so that as I approached the end of the tunnel I could feel a buzzing in me that was not entirely due to the danger that might be lying ahead.

I thought of the use her mouth was probably being put to, the number of cocks that would come in there. I imagined the sweet orifice of her sex being stretched to the limit by the oversized members of a dozen or more of them. They would screw her and keep on screwing her, I thought, until everyone of them had been satisfied.

A brief image flashed in my head of the young girl's soft white body, spread-eagled and tied down, plaything for dozens of sexually insatiable men...

The tunnel had stopped.

Right there, in front of me, it came to an abrupt halt, and a solid stone wall blocked my path.

I raised the torch high above my head and looked for any chinks or openings, anything that might indicate that there lay something beyond its solid surface.

The seamless face of the wall provided no clues of any kind.

"Hell's teeth," I said softly to myself. This was not what I had expected, though my brief stay in Soames' villa had taught me at least to expect the unexpected if nothing else.

I moved my torch this way and that, looking for slight depressions on the smooth wall, scuff-marks perhaps or else rings or buttons, anything that might indicate that here was a way to activate whatever doorway was hidden in the wall.

That there might be nothing of the sort was a thought I didn't really want to entertain. To have done so would have meant giving serious consideration to the possibility that Malakai might have betrayed me. If all this was an elaborate part of Soames' plan against me, I was lost indeed.

Uncertain of what exactly I was looking for, my left hand flat against the wall and searching, I must have tripped some kind of hidden mechanism by mistake.

There was an almost inaudible click. Then there was a soft humming noise and a panel, roughly square, slid back. I stepped back in delight and saw that a mirrored window had opened in the wall itself.

It was, I realised instantly, a look-through mirror, not unlike the ones Soames himself had introduced me to on my first night in this place.

On the other side was Melissa!

Hardly daring to breathe, I watched transfixed.

The room beyond was oblong.

There was no bed anywhere and the lighting was provided, as almost everywhere in Soames' expensive villa, through the use of thick stemmed candles.

Melissa, I saw instantly, had been stripped naked.

Her hands had been shackled by the wrists. Thin black chains extended from each one to somewhere towards the ceiling, stretching her arms wide and making her proud full breasts rise even higher.

She was on tiptoes.

Slowly I moved towards the thin glass separating me from her and saw that her legs had been subjected to a similar fate. Her ankles had been shackled by large metal rings and pulled apart, so that she was spread-eagled and vulnerable. The lips of her sex were red and glistening wet from the recent abuse she'd been put through at the auction.

Her head was bent forward onto her chest. Her long black tresses fell over her face and the upper slopes of her flawless breasts.

She was, I thought, the perfect picture of defeat. Lost to me. Lost to herself. Lost to the world. She probably thought that Soames had further abuse in store for her and no one to save her from him now.

I meant to prove her wrong.

But first I had to see what I was up against.

From the far side of the room, almost out of my line of sight, a door opened silently and in came Edward Soames. He had changed into an open-necked silk shirt of brilliant white and loose black trousers and boots.

In one hand he held a riding crop and as he walked towards the helpless Melissa he kept tapping it impatiently against his boot.

When I'd first watched through the mirrors on Soames' insistence, I remembered him saying how I had to keep quiet. How he hadn't had time to sound-proof the mirrors. As I stood silently on my own, behind one now, I remembered what he had said and breathed shallowly to avoid making even the most basic of noises while I listened.

"So you thought that helpless journalist could help you?" Soames said as he walked behind Melissa.

If she heard him she didn't respond. She remained as she was, tied-up, spread-eagled, vulnerable - and silent. Sexy and yet defiant. Totally at his mercy, probably about to be abused again, and still managing to project an admirable quality all of her own.

It was a fresh reminder why I was here still. Why I so badly wanted to beat Soames. Why I wanted, above all, to see him destroyed.

"You thought you could leave me, is that it?"

No answer.

"Well, you'll be pleased to hear that your little boyfriend has failed."

Still nothing from Melissa.

Standing behind her, Soames put out a hand and touched her ass. The full round buttocks, slightly pulled apart from the awkward position her legs were in, fitted neatly into the palm of his hand as he hefted them one at a time. He squeezed the soft smooth flesh, and, appraising it with an expert eye, measuring the depth of punishment he was about to meet out to her body.

Soames had stopped talking.

His hand instead began to move about, make its way on the smooth curves and plains of Melissa's naked body. From behind, it travelled down the full round cheeks of her magnificent ass, went between her spread legs. His palm flattened itself against her sex, trapping both lips of her labia.

Slowly the hand squeezed.

Melissa's head flew up, eyes open.

"Liked that, did you?"

His hand squeezed again and Melissa in vain tried to move. Then he rubbed his open hand back and forth along the lips of her sex, forcing them to involuntarily part in response. The action also made Melissa's breasts heave up and down as her breathing grew heavier. Soames continued to rub his hand between her spread-eagled legs, the movement becoming more vigorous, and I saw a glistening trail begin to coat the palm of his hand as Melissa's voluptuous body unwittingly responded to her master's caresses and began to secrete her love juices.

"Bitch!" Soames hissed, and withdrawing his hand from between her legs he slapped Melissa hard on the ass. Her naked buttocks shook with the force of the blow and she bit her lips to keep from crying out.

"I should sell you!" Soames said to her, and I felt my fears rise up inside me. "But it's more than you deserve. Instead I have another fate in store for you. Something special," he said.

As he spoke he went close to her again. Still standing behind her he snaked his hand round her body, over her hips, up her rib cage to her breasts. His hand eagerly cupped and squeezed each of her lush globes. He squeezed and stroked her nipples, almost gently at first, then harder and harder, rubbing the firm, heavy flesh of those incredibly perfect mounds.

Arousing her.

Indeed Melissa's well-trained body responded instantly to his touch. She arched her back, came up even higher on her toes. Her head shot back, her mouth opened.

Soames savoured the special feel of her exquisite body, her perfect skin. Tied-up like this she was completely his. His toy, his chattel, to do with as he pleased.

And he meant to use her.

His fingers snaked themselves between the deep valley of her breasts, up the slender pillar of her neck, over her chin to her full-lipped mouth.

I watched Melissa part her lips and suck Soames' fingers in. Her smooth cheeks hollowed with the sucking action, and I wondered again at the strange hold this cruel man seemed to have over her.

As she sucked and licked his fingers, Soames brought his other hand into action. He held the riding crop like a sword, and as Melissa worked her mouth on his fingers he slid the polished length of the riding crop up and down her legs, rubbed it against the sleekly smooth inside of each of her thighs.

The tip of the riding crop moved incredibly slowly, up the soft part of her inner calf at first, past the knee, onto the inside of her thigh, riding the gentle curve of her tender inner thigh until it reached its peak between her legs. It stayed briefly at the junction there, casually rubbing against the raised lips of her labia, careful not to touch her in between.

Then, as if it possessed a mind of its own, it moved round to caress the tight curve of Melissa's full buttocks, the deep cleft in between.

It snaked round the rim of her anus, forcing it to tighten in reflex, then up onto the small of her back, down onto the plump raised surface of her other buttock and down again, riding its sharp curve to the smooth inside of her thigh.

Melissa suffered all this attention in stoic silence, her mouth working on her master's hand, content that as long as she didn't complain her punishment was not forthcoming. Hoping perhaps that Soames would be satisfied with this show of ownership and let her be.

But Soames before long tired of his play.

He pulled his fingers away from her mouth and stood back to admire the view her spread-eagled body presented him from the back.

"A little lesson then my vixen," he said, and I felt my heart sink. "A little lesson to remind you who is your true master."

He went to a table by the far wall and from there he picked up the biggest, thickest dildo I'd ever seen. It was made of smooth black onyx and was wickedly curved to imitate a penis. As Soames produced it, Melissa craned her neck to see what he was doing.

"Yes," Soames said, approaching her again from behind, "a lesson you won't forget in a hurry."

"Please master, please." Melissa's throaty voice was tinged with desperation and I felt my heart go out to her.

"You'll be begging for far more in a minute, you slut!"

Soames was obviously in no mood for forgiveness. He reached out and touched the bulbous tip of the black dildo onto the middle of her naked back, between the twin ridges of young muscle running down her spine, and Melissa pulled and thrashed at the chains holding her.

The pulling of her chains made the tight round mounds of her ass shake in a delightful manner and as her full breasts bounced and joggled with the movement it all added to the delectability of her body.

Soames ran the dildo down her back. Reaching her round behind he forced it between the tight cheeks of her buttocks, its glistening head parting the deep cleft between them, and momentarily poised it threateningly over the round rim of her ass.

Then, as if having changed his mind, he proceeded to push it down further, until it rubbed at the exposed lips of her labia, its head parting the plump depilated folds. Then he changed his grip on the dildo. He dropped his wrist and hesitated a moment. Then, with a deft half-twisting motion of his hand, he thrust the bulk of the black dildo deep inside the soft warmth of Melissa's defenceless body, burying it inside her to the hilt.

He stepped back to admire her.

With her legs apart, her pussy lips splayed by the black monstrosity Soames had shoved inside her, Melissa flailed silently.

The end of the dildo stuck out of her so that her as her inner muscles squeezed and moved against the polished onyx, her love juices ran down its length and coalesced into iridescent drops that fell from its blunt end onto the floor.

Not yet satisfied with what he'd done, Soames now brought his riding crop into play. With a swift blurring motion he cut the air and lashed Melissa's round ass.

The shock made her cry out, but again he raised his hand and lashed her on her behind, marking a red furrow a full inch above where he'd struck her before.

Now there were two raised welts on Melissa's full behind. The plump cheeks marked above and below by the path Soames' riding crop had cut. Indicating, in between, the area he meant to strike next, before he used his other tools on her or plowed her rear with his member.

Having admired his handiwork Soames then proceeded to

lay in full measure into Melissa's exposed buttocks. He took full swings, bringing the polished length of the riding crop full strength down onto her delectable ass, delighting in the sharp hiss she made each time and the way her ass cheeks bounced and shook with the force of each fresh blow he landed.

His enthusiasm for this work grew so that his face took on this glazed expression and his hitting arm exerted itself more and more, marking Melissa's cream chocolate coloured flesh with dark red welts.

"A little lesson you bitch, a little lesson," Soames panted as he wielded his riding crop with renewed vigour, attacking her ass with a zeal that told me he'd done this to her before, that indeed this was but a prelude to far greater agony she was about to be subjected to.

It was as if Melissa expected it too. She tried to keep from crying out, tensing her body as much as she could to absorb the pain. The hiss that escaped her was the only indication that she was in such pain.

At length, Soames finished and came up close behind her t spend a few brief moments admiring his handiwork on her ass. Then he reached out and with a quick motion that tore a cry from Melissa's lips he gripped the moist end of the dildo protruding from her cunt and pulled it out.

Then he whipped his hand around the front of her body, unerringly found the opening of her mouth, and thrust the dildo in to the hilt, effectively gagging her. Then with his left hand he found the opening of her anus with the head of the riding crop, and worked it in until less than half the length of it was left sticking out.

With her mouth full to capacity and her back passage occupied by the riding crop there was only one of Melissa's orifices that was left spare and Soames had plans to take care of that. He moved up behind her, dropped his trousers to reveal his full erection, and without hesitation plugged her last remaining orifice with the full length of his cock.

Melissa tried to cry out as he rode her, his hands alternatively squeezing her wide hips or roughly crushing the fullness of her breasts. All she could do was to make a muffled half-gagged sound that got weaker and weaker the longer Soames went on.

Then, with a jerk that tensed his entire body, he was spent. He pulled his member out of Melissa's glistening pussy, its lips coated with her mingled juices and the thick white globules of his come and stepping away from her he quickly put his attire in some order. I thought that he had finished, but I was wrong - Melissa's 'lesson' was far from over yet.

He strode purposefully to the door across the room and swung it open.

"Gentlemen, come in," he said, and I felt my heart sink in sympathy for Melissa. "She's all warmed up as I promised."

In stepped two fat businessmen. They were dressed in navy pin-stripe business suits and ties which precluded them from having been part of the crowd of the auction. The younger of the two had an expression on his face that boded ill for Melissa and both almost drooled as they saw her perfect body, tied-up and spread-eagle, displayed and helpless.

They took instant stock of her full round ass and the riding crop sticking out her anus, the open lips of her cunt. And then the shorter, fatter one, who was also the ugliest, went round to see her breasts. The sight of those perfect orbs, coupled with Melissa's helpless expression at the dildo stuck in her mouth, almost made him come on the spot.

"That'll do Ed, that'll do," he kept on saying, gleefully rubbing his hands together.

"She's yours for an hour," Soames said. "No more."

"An hour's fine!" the younger one said, and they both waited until Soames had left the room before they turned towards Melissa and circled her like vultures at a feast.

"Nice piece of ass," the younger one said, experimentally twirling the end of the riding crop still stuck up Melissa's anus.

They both laughed at the muffled cry this action produced.

"Nice cunt," the fatter one said, slapping his hand between her open legs, and again they laughed as Melissa half-moaned.

"And look at these tits!" They were in front of her now, admiring her breasts, their grubby hands crawling all over her.

"We should breast-fuck her perhaps," the fatter one suggested.

They were both shedding their clothing to reveal smooth hairless bodies, bulging bellies, and soft legs.

"Soames said we weren't to untie her," said the other.

"Yeah, but Ed ain't here." The older one hopped one-legged out of his trousers. "We untie her, mouth-fuck her, have her suck us till she half-chokes, then we tie her up again. No problem."

His friend seemed unconvinced, but as he looked at Melissa's naked body a half-dreamy expression crept over his face and he dryly licked his lips.

"Butt-fuck her too," he said. "I'd like to stick it to her from behind."

"Why not?" the other agreed. "We can do anything we like, right?" He reached out for the riding crop and pulled it out of Melissa's anus and they sandwiched her between them, getting in position for action.

While one stuck his shaft into her and started shagging her violently from behind, the second suckled her breasts, his face buried between her full globes. He pinched and rolled her nipples between his fingers in a frenzy and struck her now and then with the riding crop across the smooth flat plain of her belly.

Unable to cry out, her mouth filled with the black dildo, Melissa stoically put up with the abuse, waiting for them to finish using her.

Now they changed position. The younger one used the riding crop to tease her nipples while his older companion shafted her from behind, his cock pushing up the tight bud of her ass.

The younger man reached forward and seized hold of the black dildo and slowly pulled its glistening length from Melissa's mouth. "Look at the size of this," he said to his companion who had his hands clawed into Melissa's ripe hips and was straining against her, his face contorting with each thrust up her anal passage.

"Wait, wait," he panted, and pulling his stunted but erect member out her ass, he pointed at the pouty-lipped opening between Melissa's spread-eagled thighs, "There, stick it there, now. Shove it up her cunt."

The young man complied instantly, shoving the dildo to the hilt into the central opening of Melissa's body.

Her mouth now freed, Melissa cried out at this new invasion of her much abused private parts, but in vain. Her cries further inflamed the two degenerates, so that as the younger one kept thrusting the dildo in and out of her pussy, the other rose on tiptoes and buried his penis into the tight opening of ass again.

Melissa was trapped, a live flesh sex-toy, warm and responsive, completely at their mercy. I watched helplessly as they started afresh on her, releasing her arms from the chains that held her, but keeping her feet chained up, legs far apart.

They bore her down on the floor between them. One held both her arms above her head, while the other mounted her and began to thrust against her cunt. Her screams and cries made them both laugh as they took hold of her legs next and raised them up, bending the knees until they almost touched her shoulders, fully exposing the twin well-used orifices of her anus and cunt.

Then they began again in that position.

Holding her down on her back, the older one knelt by the side of her head so that the bulbous tip of his erection brushed against her cheek. He sized hold of her hair and turned her head towards him. Then he threw himself upon her and thrust his penis deep into her hot warm mouth and began to pump it and in and out.

Melissa made half-choked sounds as the man on top of her face mouth-fucked her, while the other thrust himself in and out of her cunt.

Then the one deep in her mouth went rigid and choked back a cry.

I watched as Melissa's throat worked to swallow the squirts of semen splashing inside her cheeks.

Almost simultaneously the younger man between her legs arched his back, hips thrusting forward to drive as far in her as he could get, and let out a mighty cry.

They were done with her. Moving rather tiredly they disengaged themselves from the prostate body of the girl they'd just fucked. I watched them as they put on their clothes. Their faces were a picture of bliss.

Melissa lay still, on the floor, unmoving. She was on her back. Little flecks of semen staining her full lips at the corner and more droplets still, hanging like white pearls against the coffee-coloured skin around her well-used labia.

I watched as the two loathsome creatures left the room and I guessed they were going to find Soames, to tell him how satisfied they were.

Unable to help the girl I so desired, I hid my face in my arms. "Soames, you bastard. I'll get you!" I said through gritted teeth.

And at that moment, though I didn't know how and I didn't know when, I really did harbour a fierce desire to wreak vengeance upon the Englishman that went far beyond my desire to beat him at his own game and steal his girl.

Lying there, like that, leaning on the glass mirror, watching the rise and fall of Melissa's bruised breasts, the bite marks and scratches upon them a sign of the ill-use she'd just been subjected to, I was unready for the heavy hand that fell upon my shoulder.

I jumped with fright, stifling a scream that instinctively rose towards my lips and as I turned I saw the dome-shaped head of Malakai, his hard visage inches from mine, a thick finger upon his lips in the universal sign for silence.

My surprise was total. Not only had I not heard the brute approach but he was carrying in one hand a short-handled broad-headed axe.

I watched with eyes wide as he tucked the axe in the wide belt that held up his trousers and said: "Quiet, no any noise if yar to surprise the Mastah."

I couldn't believe my eyes.

"I come to help," he grinned. "Blondie girl good. Her service us all."

"The blonde girl? Soames exclusive sex mistress?"

"Her servicing still, long day," he showed me his white teeth.

So I'd been right. The servants had put the blonde girl's body to many an inventive use. With that thought came the realisation. There would be no going back for them! When Soames found out his anger would be terrible.

Malakai, of course, was as aware of the narrow possibility of choices left to him and his compatriots as I suddenly was. It explained his presence there.

With an axe!

"You're rising up against Soames," I stated.

The dome-shaped head nodded.

Heart thudding I turned back to the mirror through which Melissa's beautiful body could be seen. "You know how to get through this?" I asked.

Malakai contemplated the scene beyond the mirror for a second. His eyes took in the marks on Melissa's body, the signs of wild unrestrained sex and his gaze scanned the room beyond.

"They're gone," I said. "But Soames will be back any moment,"

The mention of Soames' name galvanised the giant into action.

"You defeat the Mastah," he said.

"Let me worry about that, get Melissa out of there."

I held my breath as Malakai turned back to the wall, studied it briefly for a moment, and then depressed an area right in the middle of it.

There was a brief click and an entire section of the wall slid back.

I was about to go through and pick up Melissa in my arms. Tell her that her ordeal was at last over. That I was going to take her away from her evil master. But Malakai's heavy hand on my shoulder prevented me.

"Go!" He urged. "Mastah come to see ya, yar room. Malakai watch after Melissa. Go!"

10

I was working from memory now as I re-traced my steps down lengthy corridors of every description, all part of the villa complex Soames had put together.

I passed smokeless torches and strange-smelling rooms. I

passed strange configurations of doors I couldn't even remember from before, doors that led off rooms in clusters of three and four, or else seemed to lead into strange rooms no bigger than a cupboard. I passed a couple of Soames' brown servants - this time they met my eye, nodded to me in acknowledgement, and pointed with their bony fingers, showing me which way to go.

My feet took me past the door which led to the room where I'd found by mistake Soames' special girl and thus got things rolling.

I fancied I could hear muffled moans coming from inside, the muted slap of flesh on flesh. My curiosity made me stop and turn back. I put my hand on the polished handle and slowly opened the door a crack.

Sure enough the girl was there.

She must have cried a lot. Her eyes were red and swollen and her lips had the ruby-red look of someone who'd bitten them a lot against the pain, or else had been forced to suck a lot of cocks. She was on all fours and facing the door when I peered in. Naked. Her pert cone-shaped young breasts with their pink nipples pointed at the floor and were bouncing back and forth.

A strong-looking stud knealt behind her, his massive hands hooked on her slim hips. He was pumping her from behind and, judging from the tightly screwed-up expression I could see on the girl's face, probably stretching her rear passage.

On the bed lay another three or four naked men. They were watching, waiting to take their turn with her.

Fair enough, I thought. Soames had abused their women for a long time. I thought of his cruel treatment of Melissa, the things he'd done to her, and what he had others do to her, and I didn't feel any remorse at what the blonde girl was due to get.

Because of Soames, she had it coming!

So I closed the door gingerly behind me and went on my way again, the faint moans of the blonde girl as she was buttfucked a reminder that whatever it was that I had started had already began.

My steps led me almost unerringly into familiar territory, into corridors I knew well, and without any further guidance now, I made my way back to my own room. I pushed the door open and threw off my sweaty shirt, quickly replacing it with another.

Someone had replenished the decanter of red wine on the white linen table by the wall. The same someone, I guessed, had erased the red arrow Melissa had put there for me to find, the night I took part in the masked orgy. Without the arrow, I didn't stand a chance in Hell of finding the switch that would make the wall panel slide back again. But, I decided, it didn't matter.

Not now.

Soames would come to me soon enough!

I threw myself on the bed and poured some wine into a tall crystal glass. I was bringing it to my lips when there was a knock upon the door.

"Enter," I cried, expecting Soames.

The door opened gently and there stood two of the most beautiful women I had ever seen, one brown and one white. They were dressed in sumptuous silks of a single colour, the hemlines of the fabrics that covered them trailed to the floor, and their dainty feet were bare.

I stood up, not yet too sure what to do. As usual, the unexpected had happened. It could well be that Malakai's plan, whatever it had been, had failed. Perhaps Melissa and he had been caught. Perhaps not all of Soames' servants had rebelled against their master.

"Master," the two girls spoke as one and gave me a little curtsy, "we are a gift from Master Soames."

I nodded, eyeing them up appreciatively.

The brown girl had long wavy hair fanning down to her slim shoulders, and downcast eyes that would not meet my own. Her frame was slender, long and willowy with high round breasts that were covered in white swaths of sheer silk. Through the material I could make out the merest hint of her body, its comely outline and the darker rounds of her nipples where her breasts strained against their binding.

Her lips, were full and fleshy, as is usual to those of her race, and as I admired her I recalled the bawdy tales passed round the newsroom on slow nights, when the Reuters hotline was silent and there was little enough to report.

Tales of servile women, such as this girl, discovered by my colleagues in out-of-the-way brothels all over the city, their firm flesh capable of taking great abuse without showing any signs of fatigue or ill-use, their appetites for depravity apparently inexhaustible.

Beautiful as this girl was her, white companion was rarer still, and it was to her my attention focused now. She was slender also, frail-looking almost. Her skin was the white of ivory, untouched by the Brazilian sun. Her hair was cropped short like a man's and was the colour of white ash. Her eyes, as she slyly raised them towards me, were of a pale blue, and her lips were pink.

To offset her unique beauty she was dressed in sheer black silk. It wrapped round her, moulding her body, revealing only in outline the pleasure that was there to be had if only I was willing to reach out and take it.

There was no telling how a white girl such as her had found herself cast amongst the flesh trade that came from the barrios and further afield, but white girls were rare and I could only imagine the depravities she must have been subjected to by Soames and his cronies, before she was set to service those who came here.

"Master, I am Sugar," she said softly. She spoke with an accent, Spanish laced with heavy barrio slang.

"And I am Chocolate," the dark-skinned one added.

I bade them to come in, unsure yet of what I should do next so as not to compromise my situation no matter what happened. I need not have worried. So used were they in servitude that my barest hint was a command to them. As one they complied. The door sprang shut the minute they had stepped inside.

My slowly evolving plan was to make them sit there, ply them with fruit and rich wine, get as much information from them about Soames' set up as I could. I should learn about the layout of the villa, arm myself with as much knowledge of Soames as I could.

There is no smoke without a fire and though Soames had been fairly civil up to now, at least in his treatment of my person, I had seen the glimmers that lent weight to the tales of his ruthless nature that I'd heard before I came here. I had broken into his inner circle, and that, I thought, Soames was not likely to forgive easily.

But even as I was about to decline the carnal usage of these two girls, I had the thought that they were sent by Soames or his henchmen to test me. To see if indeed I was the one responsible for what was happening amongst his former servants, and furthermore it was possible that if these two lovely creatures failed in their seduction, Soames might take out his anger upon them.

So, playing the part that was expected of me, I approached them with the knowledgeable eye of the connoisseur. I cupped the brown girl's chin and turned her head this way and that, admiring her profile and the fullness of her ripe lips. I forced a finger past those lips, gauging the depth and silky feel of her mouth. I slapped her buttocks, eliciting a ripe satisfying sound from her flesh.

The white girl was slimmer. Her buttocks, when slapped through the silk, felt nowhere as satisfying, but her elfin face had an innocence that I found oddly arousing. I longed to have her go down in front of me. I wanted to make her open her perfect pink lips and take me inside her mouth. I imagined my semen shooting out in great bursts in that mouth and splashing over her fresh young face.

Whether it was my carnal instincts that got the better of me, or the more rational thought that indeed I had no choice but to appear to go along with Soames until I could find the moment to make my move, I am unable to say now.

The fact is I turned my back to them, walked to the bed in the middle of the room, stood by it, and turned to face them.

"Come!" I said and they both hurried to comply, coming to stand in front of me, eyes downcast. They appeared vulnerable, mine to do with as I pleased, use any way I liked. I could get used to living like this with girls at my beck and call and men well-trained to do my bidding!

I stepped forward and put a hand on the brown girl's right breast. Through the soft white silk she was wrapped in I could feel the heat and firmness of it, the sweet ripeness of her pliant flesh. I squeezed hard, savouring the feel of her, and still she would not raise her eyes to look at me.

With my other hand I did the same to the white girl's left breast. Though smaller in size than her companion's, her breasts were perfectly round and high-set. Her nipples were smaller but hard, and if the innocent-looking pink of her lips was any indication, I already imagined myself suckling on the hardening pink tips of her breasts.

With a momentary clarity I thought of Melissa's body, the feel of her in my arms, and though these girls, beautiful as they were, could not match the attraction she had for me, they would be a good enough substitute for now.

"Undress me!"

I delivered this with a masterly tone, as if I had done it a hundred times before, and the two girls were quick to obey. As I stood rigidly, holding myself immobile with some effort, the brown girl struggled to unbutton the fresh white shirt I'd donned. Her fingers fumbled with the buttons. Her body, scented with roses and sweet cologne, felt hot and radiant through the thin silks that covered her.

At my direction, the white girl knelt down at my feet. Her innocent face and perfect pink lips turned up towards me in an attitude almost of worship. Her slender fingers pulled and tugged at my belt-buckle as she attempted to release my trousers.

So total was their submission to me, so complete their subservience, that it fuelled my desire to an incredible degree.

The instant my trousers were down my cock sprang out erect, demanding attention. I stood waiting for the brown girl to finish taking my shirt off and then I stepped out of my shoes, totally naked, feeling the heat between my loins and the dullness of a mad roar in my ears.

I've had my fair share of women before. I've had assignments to Borneo, Bangkok and Taiwan and at each place, for a price, I've found women willing to do almost anything to please a man. But never before had I felt the complete mastery, the total control I felt now. I could see then, not withstanding my own principles, the great attraction of owning such women.

It reinforced my belief that I, instead of Soames, could do a better social job at finding them kind masters. I stood totally naked before the both of them and motioned to the white girl first: "Disrobe."

Her hands flew over the seams of the silk covering her body and it all seemed to unravel and fall to the floor around her knees.

She had long slender legs and slim hips, like a teenager's. Her sex was bare, its vertical slit pouting, clean of fuzz, like a pre-pubescent girl's. Her apple-shaped breasts were milky white and tinged in pink, the small buds of her nipples tightly shut.

I snapped my fingers and she moved forward and prostrated herself at my feet.

I left her there, admiring the slim line of her back and the womanly flaring out of her hips, as she abased herself before me, her legs folded beneath her.

"Your turn," I commanded the dark girl, and she moved with the same grace and poise to stand at my side. Slowly she shed the white silk that covered her, one layer at a time. She had fuller breasts. Round and high. Defiant of gravity, tipped with dark, purple nipples. Her hips flared out in a sweet cradle and between her legs the hairs were trimmed short, leaving only the barest vertical hint of fuzz. It was a line of defence that could only add to the conquest, make sweeter the claiming of the prize as her secret citadel was invaded.

I bent down and wrapped the fingers of my left hand round the white girl's slender neck, pulled her upright at my feet, and turned her so that she was kneeling still, her back now pressed against the bed.

Her innocent face was turned up towards me, her full pink lips in direct line with my erect cock. Her eyes were full of an innocence that I found hard to fathom. The other girl waited whilst I positioned her properly. My swollen glans brushed against her cheek and lips as I leaned over her, and without my bidding she put out a tongue and touched the very sensitive tip of my glans.

Instantly, I slapped her. Hard.

"You do only what you're told," I said.

The shock of it made her face go even more white. Her

cheek, where I had just struck her, was a peachy red, but she didn't complain. She lowered her eyes instead and whispered a barely audible: "Yes master."

I motioned for the brown girl to climb on the bed. She sat up on her knees, facing me, thighs apart, her knees on either side of the white girl's head, almost touching her ears as she knelt on the floor at my feet.

While I worked to position them thus, my pulse was racing. With every thud of my heart my cock throbbed higher and higher and raised the pleasure of my anticipation of what was to come.

Within moments everything was ready. Leaning forward I put my hands on the brown girl's shoulders and pulled her roughly to me. I crushed her lips beneath mine, my questing tongue invading the hot cavern of her mouth.

The movement brought my hips forward and, as I had planned, my erect cock led the charge and the thick shaft shot towards the waiting mouth of the white girl at my feet. Her blue eyes widened momentarily as she felt my glans part her lips, and then she knew what was expected of her.

She bent her head to the task.

Her lips opened wide and she sucked me in as deep as I could go. I felt her tongue, warm and moist, twirl itself round and round the shaft of my cock, buried as it was deep in her throat. And as she sucked, she made a slow muffled, appreciative noise.

For a moment it got too much for her. She drew her head back, the movement restricted by the bed behind her, and then, catching her breath, she plunged forward again and began to rock herself back and forth.

In all this time the brown girl stood inert in my arms, only her mouth and lips moving as she sucked upon my tongue. But she was too sweet an armful to waste on kisses. My right arm snaked round her slim waist and my left went to cup and squeeze her full round breasts. I caught each nipple between thumb and forefinger and rolled it until it hardened in need. Then I pinched it hard, and I saw her bite her lips to suppress a cry of pain.

I cupped each breast in turn most roughly, feeling the white girl's efforts at my groin redouble as my passion rose higher. I crushed the soft sweet perfumed brown flesh between thumb and forefinger and pushed the round warm globes of her breasts together, burying my face in the scented valley in between.

As I pushed forward, the white girl at my feet made choking noises, muffled by the length of erect cock now buried deep in her throat.

I ignored her.

My right hand slid round the brown girl's body, dropped low, slid over her back, sought out the full round globes of her buttocks and cupped each tight curve in turn, fondling her ass.

Not satisfied with that, I turned her within the circle of my arms, bent her over on all fours to face the far wall, and, as the twin orifices of her ass and cunt were now exposed, I drove my longest finger forcefully into the furnace of her sex.

The dark nether lips parted easily, to expose pink moist flesh. At the same time, as my invading finger reached its limit, my thumb extended, in line and parallel to it, and plunged itself into the button of her anus. She girl let out a cry and her hips moved. Excited, I moved my fingers in and out with force, my breathing laboured, my hips bucking wildly as my cock plunged in and out of the white girl's mouth. The choking noises she made as she struggled to cope with the girth of my manhood fuelled my desire.

I felt the first rise of passion splash itself against the white girl's throat. She gurgled in a muffled way and made to pull back, but I thrust my hips forward even harder, felt her chin scrunch against the base of my cock.

A red mist floated before my eyes and sparks shot across my vision and as my right hand increased its tempo, my fingers delving in the brown girl's warm wet orifices, I heard her cry out and go all limp and I came again, violently, and this time the white girl sucking me opened her mouth wider still, and though I can not be sure I could swear that I felt her throat dilate to accommodate me.

She sucked my next burst of come into her without complaint, draining me of my excess of passion, and then as I pulled my shooting cock from her mouth, my next spurt splashed itself over her face and lips.

I watched as a pointy pink tongue shot out and dubbed at a drop of white sticky semen at the corner of her mouth.

The brown girl was lying on her face, on top of the bed, the twin moons of her ass pointing at the ceiling, and as the last drop of semen shot itself against the white girl's face and started sliding down her chin, I felt a new found clarity invade my mind and found that I could think clearly once again.

I pulled away from them then and did up my clothes.

The brown girl had still not moved from the bed and as she lay there I had a clear view of her round behind, the long sweet valley formed by her spread legs, ever narrowing until it led to the honeyed centre of her.

The white girl also had not moved. She knelt in front of the bed, her naked charms in plain view. Hot droplets of sticky semen slid down her pretty face and dripped onto the upper slopes of her pert breasts.

"Get up," I commanded her quickly, and she hastened to obey.

"Slap her ass." I indicated the plump twin mounds of the black girl's full behind.

Unquestioningly, the white girl clambered on the bed, beside the prone body of the brown girl, and at a nod from me, raised her hand and began to paddle her moon shaped buttocks.

The brown girl let out a slow moan and moved higher on the bed. Her thighs fell further apart. Her legs spread wider and her hands clawed at the sheets as she was smacked from behind with force.

It was a rousing sight, and I felt the need seize me again just as at the back of my mind, the final pieces fell into place and I had a plan I could put into execution against Soames.

It was a risky plan. One that might well go wrong. And this might be my last opportunity for sport. With that thought I undid the front of my trousers and approached the white girl on the bed as she paddled the submissive brown girl's rear. I grasped her roughly by the hips and turned her so that her own pert behind was vulnerably presented to my erect member.

As she continued to paddle the other, I pulled her forcefully back on me, and penetrated her from behind. She was smooth, hot and very tight, and I had to grit my teeth to carry on. But as I pushed harder and harder, I could feel her opening to accommodate my girth.

The walls of her vulnerable rear passage widened with each thrust, until I was buried in her to the very hilt, the soft plump cheeks of her white ass providing the perfect cushion for some vigorous rear-end fucking.

As I used her, I realised that I was changed.

The man who now was being serviced by these two girls, who enjoyed hearing the smack of flesh striking female flesh, was decidedly different from the journalist who had first come in here to seek out a story.

"Perhaps whatever happens Soames has won," I murmured to myself, and with a few final thrusts I sent a fresh spurt of semen shooting up the white girl's rear end, and then withdrew.

"Get dressed," I ordered them brusquely.

Slightly dazed with my quick change of attitude they both hastened to wrap their silks around their used bodies and hide from view the sweet charms which I had tasted so recently. The thought that I might find myself in a situation again where I could have none of this, a situation in which I would once more be forced to look at women pass me by and be unable to order them to stop with a quick nod, unable to order them to undress before me and perform whatever I desired, struck me full force.

It was a thought which now was unbearable.

It was inconceivable that having drunk deep of the nectar of this life, I would willingly choose to go back to my former existence.

As if that'd been the cue he had been waiting for, the door opened just then and Edward Soames rushed in.

Only it was a Soames unlike I'd seen him before.

His normally pristine white clothes were sweaty and stained. There was a rip high up near one shoulder and there was a mad, wild expression in his eyes.

He took in the tableau. Me adjusting my clothing, the two girls upon the bed finishing getting dressed, and looked totally confused.

"Frank," he said.

"Ed, come in." I felt totally in control.

"You're here..." his words trailed off as his eyes leapt madly round the room.

"Where else?" I asked. "Thanks for the gift." Then, enjoying the sudden change of roles, I clicked my fingers at the two girls. "You may go."

For a split second they looked indecisive, as if they might disobey me.

"Go now," I said firmly, and quickly they got off the bed, eyeing up Soames and his bedraggled clothes nervously, and pushing past me they let themselves out through the door.

Soames stared at me transfixed.

"Melissa's disappeared," he said.

I was dying to know what had happened. What was happening indeed to account for the devil's almost incoherent state of mind.

"It's you isn't it? It's you!" he said. "Those bastards out there trying to come into my villa. They're your friends aren't they?"

My heart gave a jump at his words, but I kept my face purposely blank.

Abu, I thought. Good old Abu. He'd done it at last. Only I knew that unless Abu happened to be the closest pal the Minister of Defence had, and there was an army out there, he would be no match for Soames' security measures.

No match unless Malakai had stood by his word and the guards themselves were divided. Perhaps they were turning against their master, and those coming in from the outside were finding their way in unopposed.

"Who's out there?" I asked.

Soames turned his back to me and ran a hand through his blond hair. "I wish I knew. I wish I knew. My people just keep falling back. Hardly a shot fired. I just can't understand it."

"Seems a pity," I said. "I'd been looking forward to my third day and night here."

That snapped his head back and I had his attention. "You devil!" he hissed at me. "What do you know?"

"Know?" I played the fool. "I sold you my soul remember? Sold it to you so that you'd agree to stop the abuse suffered by Melissa,"

"I did, I did!" he lied.

"At the auction you did, yes. Then you went on and whipped her ass with a riding crop and if that wasn't enough you then butt-fucked her, remember? And then, when you'd had your fill of her and had finished you let those two ugly white toads use her any way they wanted."

Soames' eyes widened in surprise and horror. "How'd you know all that?"

"When you engineer doors and windows into your building and then use them as weapons, there may come a time when they'll in turn be used against you... you happened to have a little playmate, remember? Blonde, young. Body barely yet used."

That shook him to the core.

The girl must have truly been special to him.

"Bastard!" he screamed and made to launch himself at me, but I was truly transformed. The Englishman had said he wanted my soul but it would have been closer to the mark had he offered to exchange mine for his, I think.

I stopped him with a quick chopping motion of my hand. "She was English, I think, eager to please. Particularly after I introduced her to your theories on pain and pleasure. Spanked her lily white ass until it was red, before shoving my prick up her cunt."

"Bastard..." Soames looked shocked. Deflated. But he wasn't yet beaten. Not truly. I savoured the feel of power I had over him. The reversal of roles.

"And she had such an eager, willing mouth too," I said. "Insatiable girl, I grant you."

"If you've touched her -" Soames began.

"Touched her? Oh, I think I did a little more than just touch her. But then so did Malakai, I believe."

"WHAT?"

"And he had quite a few friends with him. The moment I told them there was willing white pussy ready to satisfy their needs they just left me to do with the place as I pleased. Even showed me where a particular secret passage was, can you believe that?"

"Oh God, what have you done?" Soames asked. His shoulders sagged. "What have you done?"

"Only what you so patiently taught me I could do, you sneering, supercilious bastard," I replied coolly. "You talk about sex and power, pain and pleasure. Well your little playmate satisfied a dozen cocks as a result. Last time I saw her they were drawing lots for her, queue of a dozen men or more. She was being butt-fucked and was enjoying it."

"Oh no!" whispered Soames. He looked absolutely devastated. I have never seen a man so shaken. He crumbled before my eyes.

And then the door opened and in came Malakai, bald head and face glistening with sweat, closely trailed by Abu and the mysterious man who had spoken to me at the auction before things went so wildly out of control and my despair had culminated in this new situation we were all in now.

"Frank," Abu looked genuinely pleased to see me. "You're all right?" he eyed the grief-stricken Soames suspiciously. "Has the bastard being giving you a hard time?"

"I'm OK," I assured my boyhood friend. His face was lit up, like he was having the time of his life, and he probably was, I thought. It wasn't exactly every day that one stormed an armed and guarded citadel to rescue a friend.

"What have you done, what have you done?" wailed Soames. He was totally dazed. The news about his special girl had knocked all the stuffing out of him.

"What's gonna happen now?" Abu asked, probably voicing the thought of everyone in the room.

I'd been thinking about that. One has to be practical about these things. No sense in taking out Soames. Smash his slave-trade and sex empire and you create a vacuum, and nature, as everybody well knows, abhors a vacuum. Pretty soon there'll come someone else to fill it and it would start all over again.

"I'll take over," I said.

A stunned silence followed my announcement.

"You?" gasped Abu.

I fancied that I could do a more humane job of running Soames' empire. Still making money, but not as much. I would vet the buyers very carefully and force the brothels to improve their treatment of the women I would supply them with.

"I think I've got a slightly better social agenda than Ed here," I explained. "You see, it could be made to work. Most of the girls would happily exchange their sexual favours if they could be guaranteed a better life, with masters who will truly look after them. The money we make could be pumped back into some of the barrios to improve the lot of those unfortunates whose only choice would be the inevitable slide into drugs and prostitution."

"It could work," Abu said slowly. He sounded doubtful, but his friend Jim beamed me a brilliant white smile. "What a great idea. As you say, smashing this set up won't solve the problem. Not at all."

"But you know next to nothing about the way the slave-trade works," Abu said to me.

"Oh, I could learn," I said. "Besides, I'll have some expert advice from my chief of security," I beamed at Malakai and the massive black man looked stern. He crossed his massive arms across his chest and said: "Mastah,"

"What about Soames?" Abu enquired.

I cast a look at Malakai who nodded and clapped his massive hands.

The door opened and in came Melissa, looking more beautiful and radiant than ever.

She wore a long sleeveless white dress with a nipped-in waist. From the waist down the dress dropped in long rectangular pieces of fabric down to her ankles, and as she walked every man in the room was rewarded with tantalising glimpses of milk-chocolate coloured thighs and the sexy curve of slender calves, the kind of legs that drove men wild.

Her unbound breasts rode high and proud and as she reached us she threw her arms around my neck, pressed her long lithe body completely against me, and whispered in my ear: "Thank you."

Jim and Abu admired her body and face with wistful expressions on their faces, so they did not notice the other figure who had slipped in with Melissa, until he spoke up: "I'll take care of Master Soames," he boomed.

The man was thin. And tall. Black as midnight, but with eyes clear and intelligent.

Last time I'd seen him, he had been in a cell with two women, all covered in filth, and he'd put on a sex-show for me, while one of the women had sucked me off.

Despite what I'd become, despite all the changes. I blushed at the memory of it.

The man looked at me with eyes that said he understood.

"Master Soames," he said sneeringly, "will sample a little of his own hospitality in a cell specially prepared for him."

"No! No!" Soames yelled and shrank back, but Malakai had him by one arm and he propelled him towards this black Nemesis who took hold of him and pulled him roughly towards the door.

He stopped in front of me, his eyes stricken.

"You called her my special girl," he said, "and so she was." He pulled himself erect and spat at me. "So she was was!" he repeated. "So she was! That was my daughter!"

His daughter! If only I had known...

"Let him go," I said. It was a defeated man who walked

out. He looked twenty years older than he had done only two days earlier.

Abu was a little bemused. "Well," he said, his eyes returning to Melissa's heavenly body, as she pressed her hip against mine, "you seem to have the situation under control. And here was I worrying about you."

"I don't think I could have done it without you, Abu," I said seriously. "Without the diversion created by you outside, I don't think Malakai and his friends could have seized control so quickly."

"Oh, that was Jim here." He pointed to the man who stood next to him, grinning at me. "Jim's the Chief of Police,"

"At your service," Jim said with another grin.

I looked back at him with a choked expression on my face.

"Oh, no need to worry," he reassured me. In fact he was smiling. "We could never clean this mess out anyway. What with the drug gangs and corruption. And having you on the agenda, knowing that at least some of these people will be looked after, well, one does the best one can."

"Thanks," I said a little numbly.

"There is something you can do for us though," Jim said.

"What?"

"Well, if you no longer need us, Abu and I ought to get back to those girls. They did seem so eager to thank us properly."

Malakai's gruff reply was lost in the laughter from Melissa and me.

There was soft rhythmic music in the background.

The naked girl dancing in the centre of the ring of jumping flames was truly angelic in appearance. She was a dark slender creature, with the lithe strong legs of the trained dancer and the high full breasts of the courtesan. She had silver rings through her nipples and tiny silver bells were attached to them so that as she danced and jumped and leapt the flames glistened off the sweat coating her naked body and the little silver bells gave off tiny peels as her breasts bounced jauntily.

There was no other light in the hall than the orange glow of the leaping tongues of fire.

All around the fire, strategically positioned were girls in various stages of undress. Craning their heads forward, leaning as close as they could get without getting singed by the flames that surrounded her, were men of every age, dressed in flowing white shirts and crisp white slacks.

As the girl in the ring of fire did her act, the girls positioned all around would gradually remove an article of clothing and fling it in the flames, making them leap even higher.

Suddenly, seemingly out of nowhere, in the ring of fire appeared the familiar body of a lanky young man. He was blacker than midnight and totally naked. His body glistened with oil, and the muscles of his arms, chest and thighs writhed like snakes.

He was incredibly tall and lean and as the dancing girl gyrated and jumped he casually flicked a long arm out, coiled it round her waist, and with a casual motion he snatched her out of the air and forced the dancer onto her knees in front of him.

He held her head by the hair and with his free hand he slapped her across her pretty face.

The dancer brought her hands up in mock horror.

She prostrated herself in front of the man. Her full breasts almost touched the floor as she lowered her head in seeming fright. Her firm haunches, as she leaned forward, gave everybody a glimpse of what nestled between the firm lines of her strong thighs.

The lips of her sex briefly parted and those lucky enough to be directly behind her were treated to the exquisite view of the winking pink folds within, glowing in the gap between her legs.

Men stood on their seats. They arched their backs and craned their heads to see better.

Now the black man had the woman's face pressed in his middle, her face scrunched up against his scrotum. Then he began to rub his long erection up and down her cheek in slow motion, and as everyone watching held their breath the woman's pointy tongue flicked out and licked the length of the black man's shaft.

There was a low collective groan from the lips of the watchers and the tempo of the music increased.

The man seized the woman by her hips and lifted her up, held her almost above his head, so that her depilated pussy was at eye level to him. Then, arms trembling with the effort, he slowly brought the woman's middle towards his own lips.

Held in mid-air as she was, she spread her legs wide to accommodate him and leaned back. The twin peaks of her full breasts pointed towards the ceiling as her head arched towards the floor.

Having thus tasted her briefly, the man now pulled the woman's body down. He yanked her forcefully towards his middle and held her at such an angle that everyone could clearly see the deep penetration taking place as his long hard shaft disappeared slowly up the glistening folds of her pussy.

She moaned at the deep invasion of her body, and men craned to see what was being done to her.

All the time, the girls positioned on the outside of the ring of fire had slowly been stripping.

They now all stood naked, their charms freely on display.

I watched as a buyer approached a girl and felt her ass. He ran a slow hand over her smooth flat belly, parted her thighs to have a better look at what was on offer there, then bent his head and gently suckled from one hardened nipple as he buried his face between the pillows of her breasts.

Other buyers, the voluminous shirts they wore hiding the bulges in their trousers, approached other girls. In one instance a girl, unbidden, went down on a man she fancied and, in plain view of everybody, took his root into her mouth and to the delight and encouragement of those watching proceeded to service him to full completion. His come as he shot off his load spilled over her young face and lips.

Moments later a new price was chalked up next to the girl's name.

The couple within the ring of fire was working its special magic. More and more people left their seats to wander amongst the auctioned girls. More and more left them quickly after briefly sampling their charms, running careful hands over plump round buttocks, or expertly hefting and appraising delicious breasts, then went over to make their bids.

Then they would then scurry back and wait, watching, as they massaged their groins, in case someone else made a higher bid, in which case they would again have to up it, or else choose to go for another girl, and the process would start all over again then.

The sexual act within the ring of fire was reaching its own climax. There were rivulets of white semen streaking the girl's hair and face and she was being butt-fucked now while on all fours.

"It's going smoothly enough," Melissa's purry voice said from beside me. She had on a tight white dress that made it obvious that she had not bothered with any underwear. It was short, and as she stood beside me, one hand put proprietorily on my shoulder, I surreptitiously dropped an arm to the fullness of her rump, then to the hem of her short dress, and slowly up the smooth skin of her inner thigh.

Melissa's grip upon my shoulder tightened as my fingers

found the opening of her unclothed sex.

"Such a brazen display," I said, as my fingers eagerly dived within the sweet folds.

Melissa's tight pussy was hot and wet with arousal, and as I delved deeper inside, she swayed beside me.

"Do you want me to suck you?" she whispered, bending to my ear. The movement allowed my fingers easier access and she let out a low gasp at the deeper incursion into her sex.

"What about business?" I enquired, motioning with my head towards the auction.

Melissa's honey brown eyes locked onto mine and she ran a lascivious tongue over her lips. "That's business. I'm talking pleasure."

I slid my hand out of her sopping wet pussy and ran it up and down her ass.

It was a magnificent ass. Smooth, firm, tight.

Her whole body was like that, an instrument of pleasure that only I commanded.

I nodded to Malakai, who stood by the furthest wall, his arms folded across his mighty chest. He was making sure that everybody stuck to the new rules, and no girl was forced to do anything against her wishes.

"Stand in for me," I mouthed quietly, and Malakai's massive dome head nodded in slow motion.

I stood up, unnoticed by the glassy-eyed buyers, their attention riveted on the exquisite girls on display, and taking Melissa by the arm I led her through a secret panel in the wall to a room I had only just recently discovered.

In the middle was a massive round bed and attached to it were wide leather straps. There was also a black leather mask that would cover the entire head but leave openings for the eyes and mouth, and a black leather whip.

"Why Frank, what a surprise!" Melissa purred beside me.

I grabbed her and forced her onto the bed. Her dress rode

up around her waist as she pretended to resist, and as her depilated sex became exposed I lost all control and flung myself on top of her.

Pushing her legs apart with my knees, I seized her marvellous breasts and squeezed them through the thin fabric of her tight dress.

"Tie me up, tie me up first," Melissa was gasping beneath me, but I was already buried deep inside her body and as I started banging away, I thought dimly that bondage would come later. Her hands played wildly at my back, pulling up my shirt to feel my body, her sharp nails raking the exposed skin of my back as I pumped her.

"Put your legs up," I mumbled, head buried in the sweet orbs of her breasts.

"Undress me first, tie me up," Melissa gasped, but she brought her legs up near her shoulders, giving me deeper access to the sweetness of her body.

Frantic now, I pinned her arms above her head with one hand while with the other I tore a strip off her dress exposing her perfect breasts.

"Tie me up Frank!" she pleaded as I plundered her, my roving hands and mouth and lips searching and finding new delights in the haven of her beauty.

As Melissa began to cry out beneath me, I reflected happily that for me another night of ecstasy was just beginning and as it was a master's prerogative, I was forcing my attention on a warm female body.

The leather straps and the whip would come fully into their own later, when the night grew old and the fierce lust that drove me became a little more refined.

A night of naked plunder was just beginning...

NOW FOR OUR BONUS PAGES:

This is the second instalment of the revised and expanded version of ERICA:PROPERTY OF REX by Rex Saviour which is now out of print.

We continue where we left off in
PLANTATION PUNISHMENT and will continue in
SELLING STEPHANIE next month.

I saw tears in her eyes as I took the slipper from her - it was a pretty solid one with a good leather sole. She manoeuvred the towel across my lap, then wriggled across me with her head to the left, cheek to the counterpane, one blue eye apprehensively on the slipper, peering through that fine glossy tumble of red hair.

Not red, I realised. Not bright red, not gaudy. I think red-gold is the correct description. Or maybe auburn. I don't really know.

I put my left hand under a small firm breast and raised the slipper in my right. Was it my imagination, or was the nipple hardening?

I paused, rather disconcerted, with the slipper in the air. The nipple was definitely rising even as the body tensed, waiting to be struck, and the breath was sucked in. Surely that that should not happen? I nipped the nipple suddenly, and it stiffened even further between my prying fingers. Was the little minx reacting like this to abuse?

Anyway, there was no need to hurry. It was pleasant, holding the slipper aloft and admiring the way her buttocks contracted and she tensed and held her breath so long.

"The way your arms are tied," I said. I was beginning to realise how high up behind her back they were secured, straining her whole body to be very upright and offering those neat little breasts to me so agreeably. "A bit elaborate, isn't it, even if this Uncle Willie of yours was a sailor?"

She wriggled even more delightfully.

"Oh, but it isn't just while I wait to be punished," she said. There were tears in her voice. "I told you - he likes to keep me like this! I told you!"

She had said something, but I hadn't really taken it in, not the full horror of it.

"It's three days since he did it this time," she said. "Since I stole the money."

"What? That was three days ago?"

"He ties me up for just anything and Rita couldn't care less. She says I'm less trouble tied up. Once they had me like this for - for weeks!"

"My God!" I said. I would apologise to the Lord later! "But - what about -"

"Willie comes and cleans me up," she said. "I have to ask him nicely, but I hate to be dirty and smelly." She was blushing beautifully. "And he baths me and, and powders me, and rubs scent into me, and brushes my hair, and makes up my face, eye shadow and lipstick, you know, he likes me to be pretty, like as if I was a doll. HIS doll! And he enjoys me having to beg him to feed me..."

I was so worked up that I brought the slipper down that first time far harder than I had intended, as if it was this Willie of hers I was hitting. I heard her suck in her breath, and her body jumped, then she settled back, biting her lip, tensed for the next blow, bare bottom twitching, tears overflowing when I put the slipper down for a moment and turned her head up by twisting a hand into her hair so that I could look into those frightened blue eyes.

"He shouldn't keep you tied up like this," I said, "or do those other things to you, but stealing IS a sin."

No reply. She was biting her lip harder, and blinking back the tears.

"So is blasphemy!"

"Oh God!" She jumped and looked up at me in horror. "Oh God, I didn't mean to upset you, I mean, I'm sorry I mean! Oh - oh - oh God!"

That did it! I gave her a slippering which ended up being much more severe than I had intended. She soon started to squirm so deliciously on the towel over my penis that I hot harder and harder, and I felt her nipple in my palm, hard as a rock, as her bottom became pinker and she began to whimper, then burst into stifled sobs.

I worked myself into a frenzy of blows on those writhing bare buttocks, harder and harder, until I finally came, my seed squirting obscenely into the towel, soaking my flesh and hers, yet it was followed a few minutes later, entirely on her initiative, by a pressing squirming body coming up my chest and a kiss that was both sweet and precocious, open mouth and active tongue. I think both were entirely innocent, except in my disturbed mind.

One thing, though, that did trouble me about it, and also somehow made the kiss more erotic - I got the feeling that it was forced, that doing it was hard for her, something she felt she had to do but which gave her the creeps, and it was this feeling that began to rouse my lust again.

It was that unwanted arousal which finally opened wide a door to the cellar in my mind, gave me an overwhelming desire to beat her again and again. The monster I secretly feared was freed from the dark twisted depths of me: now we each had a monster to haunt us.

Strange, isn't it, that the sin of lust should blossom then? Was it because I had feared it? Was it because Erica was so helplessly in my power? And could it also be true that it planted the seeds of love in me, for I truly believe that the moment the slipper first cracked down across her quivering naked buttocks, or maybe the moment I felt her nipple harden under my palm, such a surprise, that was when I started to love her.

Time had passed. She had controlled the worst of her sobs and was whispering through her tears as she lay across my lap -

"You're nice. I like you, Uncle -"

"Rex." I was trying to recover my poise. After all, she was

still a naked girl with her arms bound up her back almost to her neck, and she was squirming and wriggling closer to me, now it seemed she was nestling into my arms as if she belonged there, and, believe it or not, she was smiling through her tears, like the sun peeping out after a thunderstorm.

"Will you really take me for a ride in that beautiful car, Uncle Rex? Shall I really see the seaside? And the country and cows? Oh, could we? Anywhere away from here for a little while. Oh, I do wish it could always be you who punishes me, you're so loving."

Loving! She had thought that assault loving! "We'll have to see," I said. "It would be better if you didn't get into trouble so much."

"Oh, but there's always something." She looked at me with a strange expression in those mysterious blue eyes, still full of tears but sparkling somehow, shining with excitement, looking at me so seriously.

"Would you like to know something?" she whispered.

I nodded.

"Something I've found out about myself?"

I nodded again.

"It's kind of weird!"

"Go on."

"Well, look, you mustn't get your knickers in a twist if you let yourself go a bit. With the slipper, I mean. It was alright, you see."

"Alright?"

"Yes, yes, I think I liked it, yes I did, I really liked it, it gave me such a funny feeling - warm, a glow, I can't describe it -"

"WHAT!"

"Yes, I think I might enjoy being punished if it was always you who punished me. But not Uncle Willie - oh God I absolutely LOATHE being punished by him, even touched by him - oh God oh God oh God, not him - but if you spank me ... well, you're nice, Uncle Rex, aren't you, and somehow it was nice!" She smiled shyly, and blushed, looking down. "It's made me all wet - down there."

Did I have a masochist on my hands then? Or was it the Devil being subtle in his tempting of me?

"Of course," she said, seeming to be discovering things about herself as she went along, "I must carry on as if I really HATE it, cry and stuff!"

"I see," I said. But I didn't, not really, and I suppose she could tell.

"Or no buzz!" she explained.

I think buzz meant excitement, possibly even sexual excitement. Disgusting!

The temptation of her! The sheer temptation of her!

"Oh God, listen!"

Voices downstairs.

"It's Uncle Willie, don't let HIM beat me, don't let him touch me, Oh God how I loathe him, I totally loathe that man, being touched by him gives me the creeps! - his fingers on me, ugh!"

Erica scampered for her corner as someone came heavily up the stairs. There, framed in the doorway, stood a huge black man, gross and glowering, wearing nothing but trousers over a real beauty of a beer belly.

He walked to the bed and picked up the broad leather brass-studded belt that hung on the wall beside it. "What the fuck!" he said, doubling it up and thwacking it into his palm.

I stood up. "I've given Erica her punishment for today."

"No fucking way!" He was really furious. "Little bugger wouldn't be on her feet if you done it proper. I gotta finish the fucking week or you piss off, see? She said, Rita, Erica's mum, she said."

I heard a muffled sob from Erica, standing naked in the

corner with her back to us, shoulders strained back, arms bound so high behind her back, on tiptoe now with her legs wide apart.

"Wait," I said to Willie. "This won"t do." I don't suppose I spoke with any conviction: he seemed like six feet four and bulging with muscle as well as fat and I am no hero.

"Piss off!" he snarled. "OK, so you got the fucking cash, you the big cheese while you flash it around, but I got some rights still an don't you fucking forget it man I'm your neighbour so you better be careful. Don't try squeezing me right out, I'm pretty solid wid Rita! Bottle o' whisky now an' then and a good screwing, that all it take."

"You enjoy hurting this girl!" I exclaimed.

He grinned at me as I pulled my trousers up. "So what? Sure, I dig her real good. Big Willie ain't got much goin' for him, but he gonna enjoy her the rest of his week. You wanna watch me fuck her after I beat her, new boss-man? She really hates that, screams her head off usually!"

He was taking his trousers off: Big Willie stripped was a gross sight indeed. He laid himself down on the bed and spread his legs, his penis standing up like a great rod, purple tipped, dribbling at the end, obscenely swollen.

He winked at me and clapped his hands loudly.

Erica turned at once and started to walk gracefully but ever so reluctantly towards the bed, head up, chest out, slowly and on tiptoe as he must have taught her. Then, suddenly, she threw herself at my feet and raised a tearful face to me as I stood there half-dressed, her breasts against my open trousers.

"Don't stay, Uncle Rex. Please don't stay."

"Wouldn't it help?"

"No, no, if you watch he'll be worse, ever so much worse. he always is, he likes to show off what he can do to me!"

"Come here you fucking little bitch," shouted Willie, and

her flesh trembled against me. I felt her hair on my feet and then a quick sweet despairing kiss as she dropped her head to them.

"Go, Uncle Rex! Go!"

So, coward that I am, I picked up my shoes and turned away from her.

The last thing I saw as I opened the door, she was crawling very slowly up the bed between his open legs, inching towards his massive erection, tossing her long reddish hair back over her shoulder, the pink tip of her tongue already tracing a path of moisture up the inside of one bulging thigh ...

... Rita, her step mother, stood swaying at the bottom of the stairs, a salacious smile on her pudgy face, unsteadily brandishing a bottle of whisky. It was no good taking it up with her, even if she could control Big Willie, which I doubted.

I put my hands over my ears, but I couldn't blot out the sounds from upstairs as I sat at the kitchen table with Rita cackling into her glass and leering at me, despicable coward that I was.

I jumped up and rushed out of that evil house and drove around in the car until evening, trying to calm myself...

1-3

The light was on when I went up to our room that evening, and Erica lay wrapped up in a blanket on a mattress on the floor beside the bed. 'Wrapped up' is not quite right, for the blanket was too short for her.

She lay face down, only hair to be seen at the top, but most of her legs were uncovered. She was very still, so still I wondered if she was really awake and terrified of attracting attention.

Beside the bed hung the belt, Willie's favourite belt of

studded leather, but what drew my eye was a hefty riding crop on the dresser. I went over and picked it up, and its feeling in my hands gave me quite a thrill. It seemed to belong there as my eyes returned to those white legs stretched out, so still, long and slim but shapely and with a delightful swell to the thighs just as they disappeared under the edge of the tatty old blanket...

I walked over and put the tip of the crop under the blanket where it intruded and flicked it up and back over her plump little bottom, exposing half of it.

She did not move.

I rested the crop on flesh, moved it around in a little circle. Still she stayed still. Even stiller, if anything. I turned the blanket right up over her waist, and licked my lips.

Still she did not move, no attempt to pull it down.

What a beatable bottom she had!

No wonder a sadist like Willie fancied her!

It was her misfortune, that and her cheeky little face and the gorgeous long soft red-gold hair that framed it, and the supple figure that swayed about in invitation every time she moved.

I knelt beside her and prayed for strength to resist temptation, put out the light before getting undressed, for I am rather shy although I sleep nude, and got into bed.

I woke to hear her crying quietly to herself in the darkness.

"Are you cold?" I asked.

"No it isn't that, Uncle Rex. It's the dark. I'm so scared!"

"Don't cry!" I said. It was very provocative. "You'll be safe now, with me here."

She stopped at my command, but five minutes later she started again, very softly indeed.

"Be quiet," I said. "Or I shall have to spank you," I spoke

roughly, God forgive me. It would be so easy to give way to temptation.

She was quiet for another few minutes, then I heard a whisper. "Oh God, I thought I heard a s-snake."

"Nonsense," I said. Once more I overlooked the blasphemy, but the day would come when... I put the thought from me. "How could there be a snake here?"

"My Father used to put them in my bed. Now Uncle Willie does it sometimes. They look for me because I'm warm, bits of me to wriggle into, they like warm dark holes - and - and I can't stop them with my arms tied - and - and in one of the videos, they -"

"Hush, never mind that, you're safe just now," I said. "Go to sleep." I felt very inadequate: she was obviously in need of skilled psychiatric attention. I didn't dare invite her into my bed, my thoughts were so corrupt that my Immortal Soul was surely in danger.

It must have been half an hour later that I woke up to hear a train rumbling beneath the house and feel Erica creeping under the blanket at the bottom of the bed, wriggling past my feet.

"Let me come in!" It was a frightened little whisper in the dark, and warm breath on my legs. Then a tongue, like a kitten licking, coming up my thigh... "Oh please! I'm so frightened on the floor!"

Wriggling up my body...

Now she felt delightful next to me, warm and cuddly, soft lips to mine, breasts pressing against my chest, but I was determined to do the decent thing...

"What are you wearing?" I exclaimed.

"Nothing!" she said. She sounded surprised. "I haven't got anything!"

I felt her in the dark, my hands roving over shrinking flesh, exploring everywhere... she had wriggled into my arms and yet she shrunk from me, from my touch.

"And you're still tied up!" I exclaimed.

"Yes."

"Shall I untie you?"

"Oh no!" She was horrified. "Uncle Willie would be furious!"

"Alright, alright" I said, "but I really think you should go back in your own bed." Maybe I spoke a trifle gruffly, for she drew back from me. Quite different from the shrinking.

"Oh but -"

"Or you can have your own proper bed in the cellar if you want. Rita said so."

She came close again and I felt her shudder. "I'm much more frightened there. That's where the Monster looks first! Oh, please, Uncle Rex. Don't you like me?"

"Yes of course." She was pressing against me, her touch was like an electric current.

I had to wrench my mind away from the temptation of her, warm bare flesh against me, nipples scratching my chest, close in that big bed. "What was it like," I asked very quietly, "in the cellar?"

"Dark! Black dark! I think hell must be like that. There are crawly things in there!" I felt her shudder as she turned towards me. "I shall never feel safe in the dark, I shall never be able to touch a snake, never, never, never! And the Monster - oh -"

I opened my arms and she snuggled into them, wriggling close. She stayed, trembling, but at the same time I felt her flesh cringing from mine. "You must trust in God," I said, "and don't be frightened of me, I'm not like Big Willie. Is it really so bad to touch me?"

"Oh Uncle Rex, you're so nice, but I can't help it. I shall never like men to touch me, never never never, it isn't the same as being spanked - if you're going to - to hurt me, you know - let's get it over with."

"I'm not going to 'hurt' you," I said. "And I shan't spank you either, not unless you deserve it."

"I don't have to - do anything?"

"No."

"Why not? Don't you want to?"

I was more than a bit taken aback. I think she was talking about sexual intercourse. "You're too young," I said. "You'll like it when you're older, with someone you love. Go to sleep now."

"Are you saving me up for when I'm older?"

"That's an idea!"

I was joking of course, but she was not.

"Yes, yes! Please do, Uncle Rex, please do, you're so nice. when I'm nineteen, I should like it by then, that should be plenty old enough, even for you!"

I couldn't stand much more of this. "Go to sleep!" I said. "today is enough to think about."

I woke up feeling damp. Erica lay beside me, crying silently.

"Erica!" I said, "you've wet the bed!"

"Yes." Her voice was so low I hardly heard it. She scrambled out of bed and stood there naked before me, arms still strapped up behind her back. She stood at attention, like a soldier. Perhaps Willie had taught her that. "I'm s-s-sorry, Uncle Rex. Will you use the belt or the crop?"

"What?"

"To beat me with. Or there is a slipper that Willie uses sometimes. I'm always beaten when I wet the bed, ever since I was little, to stop me doing it."

"It doesn't seem to have stopped you," I said ruefully. "Fetch a towel."

She went over to the washbasin and fetched me a towel in

her teeth.

"When I was little -" She stopped, watching me dry myself. "I mustn't tell about when I was little," she said, "but beating me just made me more nervous and do it worse. But I expect you want to?"

"Why mustn't you tell me about when you were little?"

"Daddy said not to!"

"But your father is dead."

"Yes." She shivered, and looked everywhere except at me. His death was obviously something that disturbed her deeply, and I wondered if she had really done what the newspapers had suggested, pushed him down those cellar steps.

"He's dead," I repeated. "You don't have to be afraid of him any more, so you can tell me." I stripped off the bedding, turned the mattress over, and made myself as comfortable as I could, propped up against the pillows. "You're shivering. Come back in here and tell me about it."

"Then can I whisper it?" she asked. "While you hug me? It's so difficult."

"Yes, alright."

She clambered in as best she could without the use of her arms and snuggled up to me, but still I could feel the conflict in her between being comforted and her deep dislike of a man's fingers on her.

"I've always wet the bed," she said, "as long as I can remember, and Daddy always punished me for it next evening before I went to bed, as a lesson not to do it again. He would make me take my knickers off, in case they got wet in the night, and he made me wash them at the sink, I only had one pair, I had to stand on a box to wash them, he liked to see that, and then he would make me get down and come to him and then he would pull me up over his lap by my hair to smack me, you know, until I cried, and then he would kiss me better and send me to bed, it was a blanket on some straw in a corner of the living room, we didn't have a big house then, my Mum had died or something you know, anyway I didn't have a Mum or a room of my own. Well, one day my Dad had a man with him at my bedtime, they were drinking beer and playing cards you know, and this man asked what was happening and my Dad told him and he said 'oh, then she's been very naughty, hasn't she, let me punish her' and my Dad took my knickers away and then the man smacked me real hard, and then he kissed me with his tickly moustache and then he gave my Dad some money..."

She paused, her mind in the past, revolted by it.

"Next day he came again, this man with the tickly moustache, and this time he brought a present for me, all done up in ribbons, and when I opened it it was a pair of bedroom slippers, but they were too big for me. 'Never mind,' he said, 'they'll be fine when you grow up.' And he asked my Dad, does she always sleep in her daytime clothes, and my Dad said that's all she has and then the man asked me 'Did you wet the bed again?' and I said yes and after the man had smacked me hard with one of the slippers he said 'That skirt is filthy, I'll bring her a nightie' and the next day he did."

Another pause for breath and a little cry.

"They made me put it on as soon as the man arrived. It was very short, it just covered my bottom, but the man took my knickers off and said 'see, it's too long, it will get wet' and he cut it shorter so it only came to my waist. Then he made me sit on his knee and drink from his mug of beer, and he was laughing all the time, and after a while I wanted to go to the shed for a wee, but he said 'you shouldn't let her out after dark, what about the snakes' so they gave me some more beer and sent me to bed and - and - they laughed at me when I squirmed about trying not to wee but I couldn't help it - it all came out, it went all over the bed, which was damp and smelly enough already -"

She started to shudder, and it was a while before she could go on.

"It wasn't really bed wetting, was it?" she asked. "I was awake when I did it. But I did do it sometimes when I was asleep, and he beat me for that too..."

"Go on," I said.

"I know now that he enjoyed it, I didn't understand then. I can't tell you any more, not just now, maybe later." She took a deep breath. "It's a good thing he's dead!"

"Yes, but murder is a mortal sin."

"People get locked up for that?"

"They certainly do," I said. "For their whole lives."

"I don't think he was my father, though" she said, "not really, because I heard one of his friends asking where he'd bought me and how much he'd paid and he wouldn't say. Well, that's it. They beat me and - oh! they were horrid!"

"GO ON!"

"No," she said. "No, I can't!"

"You mean you won't!"

"All right," she said. She got out of bed and fetched the riding crop in her teeth. "All right, then I won't! Now you will beat me, I suppose!"

So I did. One must have discipline.

She slept in my bed often afterwards, sometimes crying in my arms when she had been beaten or worse by Rita or Willie or their friends, always both snuggling close and shrinking away at the same time, and sometimes wetting the bed.

She always fetched the riding crop after wetting the bed, and came across my lap. I quite got to look forward to it.

1-4

It was a few weeks later that I made my move. "Mrs Fernandez," I said, "how would you like a thousand pounds?"

Her greedy little eyes lit up at once.

"What do I have to do?"

"Marry me," I said. Maybe I should have written about the loss of my wife in a car crash, but it is still too painful. If that had not happened, none of this would have.

"Ah!" I could see her mind clicking over. "You want to be Erica"s father?"

"I do, yes."

"But you can do anything you want to her already and you don't seem to do nothing."

"She's too young!"

"Doesn't seem to stop other fellers!"

"I want to take her away from all that."

"A grand ain't near enough, not to take 'er away. A nice little earner, that kid. All I got left."

"You can't go on like this."

"Oh, but I can! I got the hevidence, see!"

"Evidence? What evidence?"

"About how she done for 'er Dad. How'd you think she got off? I nicked the 'ammer she hit him with, that's how! Couldn't 'ave controlled Erica like what I done without hevidence. She's scared shitless of policemen and prison, that one. Being locked up see, all her life, and she thinks prison is where the monster looks first."

I could believe that, from what she had said to me. Fear of this imaginary monster plus the very powerful claustrophobia she had, such evidence would give anyone a very strong hold over her indeed, even if she weren't already thoroughly intimidated and totally ignorant of any help there might be.

"So," I said, "she really did kill her father? You know for sure?"

"Oh yes, I were there, weren't I? I got the 'ammer an I took a photo. Wanna see?"

She went out and fetched a roll of transparencies.

"She knows she'd be locked up if I split on 'er."

I looked at the important one, Erica brandishing a hammer as she ran up behind the man.

"That is against two Commandments," I pointed out. "Exodus 20, 12, 'honour thy father and thy mother: that thy days may be long upon the land which the Lord thy God giveth thee', and 13, 'thou shalt not kill'. You should have stopped her before she sinned like that."

"Wasn't no time to think. I did shout, like, but neither one took no heed. Anyway, who'd 'a thought a little slip like that could kill a grown man!"

But she had done, and here was the proof. This was mortal sin! Probably the poor girl had not even been baptised, never mind studied the Good Book. She must be confronted with this, and punished for it. If the law was not to take its course, then her soul must be purged by chastisement.

"Was he drunk?"

"Pissed as a newt," she said. "Well - three thousand an you gets the hevidence."

"Two."

"And what about Big Willie? He'll be mad as hive of bees, likely come and do for you, if I don't stop him."

"He's had a good time," I said.

"Three thousand, an I'll see to him too."

"Two!"

She went and made a pot of tea, her usual refuge when she had to think.

"Three thou." Her piggy little eyes were shining with greed. "Three thousand smackers." She grinned at her dreadful little joke. "Smackers, see? On a plate. Yours to do what you want with. Little cow gotta be worth that!"

"Two. In cash. You couldn't use that evidence, you'd be an accessory to the crime."

"Bastard!" she said. "I'll get you for this!"

The ironic thing is, I could easily have paid her. Let that

be a lesson to you - never walk slap into trouble if you can avoid it.

4

After the wedding, a small afternoon registry office affair, with Willie as witness, we went back to Rita's house to complete the deal. I had to allow Willie to drive, because they had watched me lock the briefcase containing the money we had agreed upon in the boot and he wouldn't part with the keys.

In an effort to be nice to Rita I had bought some champagne, but once she had counted and recounted and gloated over each individual note, she and Willie started on cans of beer. They were a pretty formidable pair and more into celebrating than I had expected.

Specially Willie with Erica.

"Time to go," I kept saying, but each time Willie would flourish the car keys in front of my face and then put them back in his pocket, becoming more and more free with his groping of Erica.

"We really must be going!"

"No, no, stay a while God Man!"

An hour went by without my being able to get Erica away, and I was becoming uneasy as the riotous atmosphere soaked through the cigarette smoke and odour of slopped beer. Willie began to look more and more like a cross between an all-in wrestler and a gorilla, and drunk at that. A feeling of malign power emanated from his huge frame more strongly than ever before.

He did nothing to conceal either his dislike of me or his letch for Erica. He was kissing and fondling her as he swigged his beer. Although I had outwitted him, his manner somehow conveyed an impression of triumph.

Erica was wearing her best and only dress, a bit short and skimpy at the best of times, and things began to get out of hand when Willie took her onto his lap and held her there, touching her up all the time.

At last her self-control snapped.

"Get off, you beast!"

"Getting brave, are we?" grinned Willie.

"I belong to Rex now you pig, so you can't do that any more."

"Don't like me much, do you, girlie?"

"I hate you, I hate you, you give me the creeps!"

"Too bad, that is, we'll have to see about that!"

"Rex is my father now, so let me go!"

"That's a fucking laugh, that is! Protect you, will he? Now's his chance, then!" Willie put his hand into her crotch and he must have pinched because she squealed really loudly. She looked at me pathetically as he mauled her, but was helpless in his grasp: this was all my fault, for she was only repeating what I had told her. Rita looked on with a smirk, smoking like a chimney and guzzling gin - she had deserted the beer some time before, and Willie was on whisky now.

"Look, Willie, just one one last kiss then lay off," I said uneasily.

"The kid's getting too fucking cheeky since you come along," said Willie, as Erica squealed again, then scratched his face. "A fucking good hiding, that's what this little bastard needs!"

"That's enough," I said. "Give me my keys."

Rita roused herself at that. "Pardon?" she said. "What keys is that?"

"My car keys."

"The keys to OUR car, you means? Are we man and wife or aren't we?"

"OK, our car keys." Technically, I suppose, she was right. "Give me the car keys please, Willie. Erica and I must be going now."

"Going, eh? You and Erica?" Rita drew herself up to her full height. "But Dearie, isn't it the bride what gets took away? To honeymoon in Jamaica or Tahiti or some such?"

A silence descended on the room. Even Erica, on Willie's knee with one of his great hands up her dress, stopped wriggling and listened.

"But this is a marriage of convenience!" I burst out. "You've had the money, Rita. You know the arrangement."

"Harrangement? What harrangement?" There was a sly grin on her face now, and a coldness gripped my guts. "You can't mean a harrangement for you to take a girl like this away from her loving mother? Buy her, like? For money, like? Lucky for you I don't recall no such harrangement, nor, I doubt, does Willie here. If you asks me it wouldn't look good."

"Look fucking bad!" echoed Willie, laughing and belching at the same time, his big paw groping away under Erica's torn dress. "Look fucking bad, that would!"

"You aren't taking me on no honeymoon, then?" asked Rita.

What could I say?

"See, you hadmits it. You don't want to consummate the marriage, as they say. I ain't good enough for you, oh no, too old I am, you goes for young stuff, you just want to take the girl away, an innocent to have your evil way with." She paused in triumph. "Why don't you just piss off, mate?"

"Yeah, man," said Willie. He jangled the car keys and put them back in his pocket with a smirk. "Just piss off, see, and we won't say no more. Rita got enough fucking dough now to go into the fucking video business again. Yeah, the kid's gonna star in more videos, I got a great idea for using the fucking snake! Look at the fucking little bitch, that's shut her up good, eh?"

"I'll take you to court!"

"Oh yeah?" Rita was grinning now, sure of her victory. "Who you think'd get custody, the mother or the man what's married 'er to get his filthy paws on the girl, had the poor thing sleep in his room already, eh? Without her own bed, even. Well, she may be so scared of you she'll say anything you tells her, but what'll anyone else believe, whatever she says?"

"Shit, forget that crap, she'll fucking well say what I tell her!" Willie put Erica head down over his knee, and, despite her kicking and screaming, pulled up the wreckage of her dress. "Gimme the fucking brush, Rita."

She waddled to the mantelpiece where a hair brush was kept and handed it to Willie with a grin. He began beating Erica's bare bottom with the back of it. She started to cry, her legs kicking wildly until he trapped them under one of his.

"Now we'll see who the cheeky little bitch belongs! Eh, God Man, what you got to say about that?"

"Leave her alone!"

"Or?"

"Or I'll make you." It sounded feeble, even to me.

"You and who else?"

It would take me and and at least two others to get her out of his grip at that moment.

The slaps of the back of the brush on tender flesh became harder and faster, but only muffled sounds escaped her, pitiful little sounds of unbearable suffering that had to be born. I think she knew from experience that screaming aloud would rouse him to a higher pitch of brutality.

"Called me a fucking pig, she did!"

She was certainly suffering for that now, and it was all my fault.

"Said I give her the creeps!"

"Don't!" I said. "Don't hit her so hard, she didn't mean it, she'll apologise!"

"Shit, man, she's been getting out of line since you come and I'm gonna make her suffer, see. I need the little cow obedient for the videos, so don't give me that crap!"

"I'll phone for the police!" I said. I looked round, but of course there was no telephone in that house. In any case it was an empty threat. Who would the police believe and what could they do?

Despite her best efforts, Erica began to scream.

"Sooner you piss off, sooner she stop howling," said Willie. He was really enjoying himself, savage in his onslaught on poor Erica's squirming bare buttocks.

I stood and watched for several moments more, rooted to the spot. My erection was embarrassing and shaming me. I was sure they were both as aware as I of the depravity I was unable to control.

At last I walked out of the house: the loss of the Rolls was nothing, but the sound of Erica being beaten followed me, penetrating my ears against my will and inflaming my own lust. Willie could be a real brute after a drink or two, and he had had more than usual today. I doubted if my leaving would pacify him very quickly.

Another thought came over me...

A beating from Willie was probably a prelude to rape.

I could visualise it all ... when he was done with the hair-brush he would grab her struggling body roughly and carry her up to the bedroom, he would tear off the remnants of her only dress and throw her down on the bed, she would lie on her back watching in frozen horror as he himself prepared, she would be too frightened to run, even if there was anywhere to run to...

1-5

Sounds and imaginings of the abuse Erica would be suffering at the hands of Rita and Willie haunted me for the next few weeks, growing in power, stirring up the dark side of my mind, bringing warped desire to the surface: I fear I spent too much time at the pub those days.

Not just any pub.

It was always busy and noisy in the raucous smoke-filled room that was the back bar of that rather unusual pub, the Fox. But it was a place where I intended to entertain Erica after I had rescued her, so maybe this is a convenient moment to introduce it.

Stephen, the rather bulky and not always genial Landlord with the oriental-looking little beard, was rumoured to have a hideout somewhere in the Far East. I was to discover later was very true - it was in the Sahdist Kingdom of Balikpan, where the Marquis is worshipped, and about which I shall have plenty to say later.

Anyway, Stephen had learnt how to attract a certain specialised clientele to the Fox from far and wide and was obviously growing rich on it.

He had started by using enlarged photographs from a magazine called Pleasure Bound as decoration, and then, one famous night, the plump timid little mini-skirted live-in barmaid, Susi, she with the innocent cornflower blue eyes and long blonde hair, spilt some beer on the floor.

The accident happened out of modesty

rather than carelessness. Maybe the men at the table she was serving had had a drop too much already. Anyway, as she leant between patrons at a close packed table she got a pinch or two on the bottom, which, being well accustomed to, she ignored, but the hands up her very brief skirt were unduly intrusive and made her jerk her arm, and over went a tray with several mugs of beer on it.

Stephen was furious. After slapping her around a little he told her to mop the floor.

"Please m-may I have a c-c-cloth?" she stammered.

"Use your knickers!" someone shouted out.

She looked at Stephen, but he just laughed. "You heard what the man said, get on with it."

There was a hush, of course, and everyone turned to watch. At first she wouldn't do it. She just stood there blushing and started to cry. But then as Stephen lifted his hand to hit her again, she hoiked up her already inadequate little skirt and slid her knickers down.

And very nice she looked too. Her thighs were nicely rounded but not unpleasantly so, a very luscious little thing.

When she had finished she started to put the knickers on again. An uncomfortable thing to do when they were so wet, but with her modesty always came before comfort.

"You can't do that!" said Stephen. "They're wet!" He handed her a hammer and nails, and made her get on a chair and stretch to fix them at a suitable height. Then she had to serve the same group another round, which soon had the whole place in an uproar.

After that it became traditional to ask little Susi to pour one's pint and get a hand up her skirt while she was doing it. Soon a row of knickers appeared beneath the pictures on the walls.

I hope I've given the right impression about Susi, calling her plump. She was plump only in a sexy way, slim waist with it, and very high firm breasts.

Then, on another famous occasion, Stephen became annoyed with her for not only squealing when a customer groped her - that had become common place by then did not trouble him - but actually complaining about it. She never complained again, because Stephen immediately up-ended her over her across the bar, head, shoulders and skirt hanging down towards the floor. He spanked her plump bare wriggling bottom for all he was worth in front of everyone. It soon went from white to red, and drew a great deal more squeals and some pretty solid sobbing from her and much applause from the patrons.

Some idiot ran out and told the police, who rushed in blowing whistles, but Susi said she deserved to be punished, it had been no big deal, and not to bother or she might lose her job with this nice kind gentleman.

After a number of such incidents the police ignored any complaints they might receive about the Fox and left us in peace. Custom built up rapidly from that moment onwards, as confidence in the security of the pub grew. One of the main reasons the place was so noisy was that the spanking of poor little Susi became more and more frequent at the same time as it became both more severe and more popular. She was undoubtedly a most attractive and spankable young person. You'd have thought she'd have got used to it after a while, but seemingly not. She appears to become more and more sensitive to pain and embarrassment as the weeks go by, which has increased the custom and no doubt the profits no end.

Stephen has to be very tolerant, of course, of somewhat - what shall we say - unusual? - behaviour on the part of some of the regulars, and not only concerning the unfortunate Susi, though she is certainly considered fair game. And the more unusual the behaviour became, and the more frequent, the more the Fox flourished.

Ladies are not permitted to sit unless invited to do so, nor to speak unless spoken to, and - a fad of Stephen's from his favourite book, The Story of O, which he goes on and on about to the point of almost becoming a bore - the tip of the tongue must always be visible through parted lips and the posture must be very erect. He enforces that with Susi, of course, but he has also been known to denounce a visiting lady for sloppiness and spank her bare bottom there and then, over the bar. If her escort does not agree, the are immediately evicted - and to go on Stephen's black list is not a deprivation to be risked lightly.

Stephen continues to slipper Susi just for pleasure these days. He has several slippers of various weights behind the bar for use on her, and is always willing to lend one out. There is no doubt that he spanks her particularly hard because she has such an inviting and sensitive bottom, and so the bar becomes noisier and noisier as well as more and more crowded, and the price of drinks has been going up and up and Stephen is getting richer and richer, buying new and better slippers for Susi.

Gentleman are expected to volunteer their lady to Stephen to assist Susi in any little jobs that might require attention, such as going amongst the customers to take orders and deliver drinks, or to mop the floor when beer is spilt, all difficult (even embarrassing) tasks in the somewhat rowdy informality of that crowded little room. These ladies are apt to suffer what is known as 'Susi's fate' if they give Stephen the slightest excuse, or if they have some special appeal for him, such as shyness - Susi is very shy, and cries a lot, which encourages the patrons to pinch or fondle her more than they otherwise would have done as she creeps timidly about her duties, trying not to attract anyone's attention - an impossible ambition, of course.

Temporary assistants have to go behind the bar to change into the correct uniform, which consists of a dog collar, a tight jumper and short skirt, garter belt, black stockings and exceedingly high heeled shoes. The bigger the girl the tighter the jumper and the taller the girl the shorter the skirt, for all the uniforms are made to fit the petite Susi, who is more desirable than tall, quite short in fact - imagining her and the extra large Stephen in bed is quite difficult, but we all presume it happens: indeed he sometimes makes Susi stand squirming on the bar with his finger up her arse whilst he boasts of his prowess, something that makes her really blush.

No knickers for visiting ladies, of course, or any sort of trouser. Short skirts without knickers are considered correct for the Fox, except the knickers Susi starts the evenings with, which seldom last long. A selection confiscated from gentlemen's guests adorn the walls, along with so many of Susi's you'd think Stephen would baulk at the cost - but no doubt the increase in trade far outweighs that. Bras are objected to less, but not considered quite the thing unless they are really necessary and have provision for the nipples to peep through.

So I would sit there fingering Susi whenever she came within reach and planning for the time when I would get Erica back, not doubting that I would do so, but knowing I must wait till Willie's alertness wore off. In this way the time passed quite painlessly.

I took some books on psychology down to the pub. Nothing useful came of this, except that Stephen borrowed them sometimes to spank Susi with, but I was reminded of an aunt I had cured of a phobia about spiders, bringing little ones closer and closer, then bigger ones, until at last she managed to reach out and touch one and was cured.

That technique is called systematic desensitization.

I purchased an expensive new text book on the subject and studied it intensively. Stephen said it was an excellent book, heavy and well balanced, and I became convinced that Erica could be cured of her hang-ups this way: what worked for spiders would also work for snakes and shyness and dislike of being touched. The Lord had showed me a way to cure her, therefore I HAD to get her back. Also, of course, it would be my duty to chastise her from time to time, to change a sinner into a truly Godly person.

I will not in future stress my own feelings so much as I have been doing: I was about to expose myself to great temptations because of a mission laid upon me that I could not in decency avoid. Much prayer had brought me to this point. Just let it be remembered that if at times I appear to be pandering to my own darker desires, that is not in fact so, for everything I now planned to do was for Erica's sake and her sake only.

6

At last the time had come, I decided, to rescue Erica.

I had drunk a lot of beer and studied the textbook on systematic desensitization in pleasant surroundings. But I had also made certain other preparations - I had put an electric fence round the estate I had inherited, changed my bank, discussed matters with my solicitor, nothing too difficult but all rather time consuming. Fortunately my telephone number at the Mansion was already ex-directory, for I have always been somewhat secretive by nature.

No way did I want Willie arriving on my doorstep, but he and Rita would not be very sophisticated when it came to detective work. I had considered taking her overseas, but I decided that was unnecessary. I had never said where I lived, not even which county, and they were too vulnerable to do anything through official channels, or so I hoped. It seemed to me that possession of Erica was nine points of the law, and I intended my possession to be absolute.

I did not buy a new car. I was quite fond of the old one, and fully intended to rescue it as well.

So, when my arrangements were complete

and vigilance would have died down, I mounted a watch on Rita and Willie's favourite pub from a cafe opposite. It was a tedious chore, involving a great intake of coffee, because although I occasionally saw one or the other it was several days before at last they arrived together, lording it in my lovely motor.

I paid my bill, strolled over to the Rolls and opened it with my spare keys. It would be noisy in the pub, too noisy (I hoped!) for the purr of the engine to penetrate. I waited to see if they would come rushing out, then pulled smoothly away. How I loved that car, the feel of the wheel in my hands was great as I drove to the house.

The front door lock had been changed, but I had anticipated that: I knew there was a suitable wrench in the tool kit. I looked round to be sure no one was watching, although people were pretty used to me around here anyway, and the car would reassure them.

Anyway, they had no love for Willie!

A splintering noise and I was in.

No Erica on the couch, but when I rattled the cellar door I heard a quick intake of breath, then a little moan.

She would think it was Willie.

The key was not in the lock.

They were not very imaginative. Within two minutes I had found it under a mat in the hall.

First thing I heard when I opened the door was a rustling noise, cockroaches retreating from the light. Then a thin keening. Erica was sitting on the top step, naked, her arms hugging her knees to her chin.

To be continued.......

TITLES IN PRINT

Silver Moon

ISBN 1-897809-03-4	Barbary Slavegirl	*Allan Aldiss*
ISBN 1-897809-08-5	Barbary Pasha	*Allan Aldiss*
ISBN 1-897809-11-5	The Hunted Aristocrat	*Lia Anderssen*
ISBN 1-897809-14-X	Barbary Enslavement	*Allan Aldiss*
ISBN 1-897809-16-6	Rorigs Dawn	*Ray Arneson*
ISBN 1-897809-17-4	Bikers Girl on the Run	*Lia Anderssen*
ISBN 1-897809-20-4	Caravan of Slaves	*Janey Jones*
ISBN 1-897809-23-9	Slave to the System	*Rosetta Stone*
ISBN 1-897809-25-5	Barbary Revenge	*Allan Aldiss*
ISBN 1-897809-27-1	White Slavers	*Jack Norman*
ISBN 1-897809-29-8	The Drivers	*Henry Morgan*
ISBN 1-897809-31-X	Slave to the State	*Rosetta Stone*
ISBN 1-897809-35-2	Jane and Her Master	*Stephen Rawlings*
ISBN 1-897809-36-0	Island of Slavegirls	*Mark Slade*
ISBN 1-897809-37-9	Bush Slave	*Lia Anderssen*
ISBN 1-897809-38-7	Desert Discipline	*Mark Stewart*
ISBN 1-897809-40-9	Voyage of Shame	*Nicole Dere*
ISBN 1-897809-41-7	Plantation Punishment	*Rick Adams*

Silver Mink

ISBN 1-897809-09-3	When the Master Speaks	*Josephine Scott*
ISBN 1-897809-13-1	Amelia	*Josephine Oliver*
ISBN 1-897809-15-8	The Darker Side	*Larry Stern*
ISBN 1-897809-19-0	The Training of Annie Corran	*Terry Smith*
ISBN 1-897809-21-2	Sonia	*RD Hall*
ISBN 1-897809-22-0	The Captive	*Amber Jameson*
ISBN 1-897809-24-7	Dear Master	*Terry Smith*
ISBN 1-897809-26-3	Sisters in Servitude	*Nicole Dere*
ISBN 1-897809-28-X	Cradle of Pain	*Krys Antarakis*
ISBN 1-897809-30-1	Owning Sarah	*Nicole Dere*
ISBN 1-897809-32-8	The Contract	*Sarah Fisher*
ISBN 1-897809-33-6	Virgin for Sale	*Nicole Dere*
ISBN 1-897809-34-4	The Story of Caroline	*As told to Barbie*
ISBN 1-897809-39-5	Training Jenny	*Rosetta Stone*

All our titles can be ordered from any bookshop in the UK and an increasing number in the USA and Austrailia by quoting the title and ISBN Or they are available from us direct for £5.60 each (UK) or $9.95 (USA) postage included. Credit Cards accepted as EBS (Electronic Book Services-£ converted to $ and back!)